THE KILLING CREED

LUCAS STONE
BOOK 3

MARK ALLEN

WOLFPACK PUBLISHING
— EST 2013 —

Paperback ISBN 978-1-63977-970-3
eBook ISBN 978-1-63977-969-7
LCCN 2022951626

THE KILLING CREED

"The scariest monsters are the ones that lurk within our souls."

EDGAR ALLEN POE

ONE

THE WAITRESS KNEW trouble was brewing when the biker followed the trucker and the hitchhiker into the restroom.

She had been waitressing long enough to spot subtle signs of trouble. Frequent repeat customers were a red flag to anyone working five shifts a week at a truck stop on the interstate. More common were those steady, once-a-month faces—cheap-suited salesmen, touring musicians, hollow-eyed hookers, and raggedy hitchhikers.

But the man wearing the red down jacket was no ordinary hitchhiker. The trucker was no ordinary trucker. And the biker was a full-patch member of the Children, which meant the kind of trouble that usually ended in bloody knuckles and broken bones.

All three had shown up nightly for the past week, but individually. Now suddenly, like volatile chemicals, they were all in the mix together. It reeked of something bad about to go down.

The waitress retreated to the kitchen. "Hey, Lou," she said to the cook. "I think there's gonna be a fight in the men's room. Want me to call the cops?"

Lou glanced up from the burger he was flipping. "What's going on?" He was a squat, powerfully built man in his fifties with two blurry Navy tattoos on his biceps and a protective streak when it came to the nice college girl who slung trays for him five nights a week.

"Three sketchy guys. They've all been coming in regular for a week. Tonight all three are here and one right after another they've followed each other into the men's room."

Lou yanked off his grease-grimed apron, balled it up, and tossed it into the corner. "Lemme go take a look. Probably a lover's quarrel."

"Really?"

"Three guys in a bathroom at a truck stop? Who says romance is dead?" Lou chuckled and shook his head. "Just keep your ears open and call 911 if you hear trouble. Got it?"

"Loud and clear." The waitress pulled out her cell phone.

Lou banged through the kitchen doors, barged through the prep area, and stomped over to the bathroom, irritated that this nonsense was messing with his dinner service. He gave two sharp knocks and then stepped inside.

"Listen, guys—"

It was as far as he got.

The biker flew across the room as if fired from a catapult. He collided with the edge of one of the sinks and folded at the waist, his head smashing into the mirror. It shattered with a jagged, cracking sound and shards skittered to the floor.

Lou spotted the trucker advancing on the biker while swinging a chain. The man in the red down jacket, blue jeans, and white cap cowered by the row of urinals.

"That's enough!" Lou bellowed. He might as well have been shouting into a hurricane.

The trucker whipped the chain around, aiming for the biker's legs. But the biker reacted faster than expected. He stepped on the chain, trapping it under his boot, and then leaned in to grasp the trucker by the lapels of his jean jacket. The biker's hard fist pummeled the trucker's face as Lou made a move to separate them.

"Cut it out!" Lou yelled. He came within a foot of the biker but then got shoved hard enough to skid backward into a trashcan. He toppled over, going down with a crash. Winded, dazed, and sucking for air, he managed to scramble up on all fours. Best he could do right now.

The biker rag-dolled the trucker, holding him upright by the collar with his left hand while hammering him again and again with his right. The trucker shuddered with each punch, the chain coiled in a forgotten pile at his feet as his face darkened to black and blue.

"Stop!" Lou croaked as he gamely dragged himself to his feet again. No way in hell was he going to let this happen in his establishment. He staggered toward the biker a second time.

But the biker was having none of it. He punched the trucker one last time, then swung him around and hurled him directly into Lou. The cook took the full weight of the man right in the chest, stumbled backward, and slipped on the spilled garbage. Hitting the ground again hurt like hell. Having the unconscious trucker land on top of him hurt even more.

God, I hope someone called the cops! Lou thought as he disentangled himself from the beaten and unconscious man. He should probably check to see if the poor bastard was still breathing. But the violence wasn't over yet.

The biker turned to the man in the red jacket and

snarled, "Your turn, you son of a bitch. Time to get what's coming to you."

The biker outweighed his target by a good hundred pounds and towered over him by at least a foot. Lou watched with a kind of dazed sickness as the biker reached into his pocket and pulled out a switchblade.

Lou fired off a prayer as he realized he was about to witness a murder. Time to get out of here while he still could.

He crawled over to the bathroom door. Rearing up on his knees, he grasped the handle just as the biker lunged at the man in the red jacket, slashing at him with the knife.

What Red Jacket lacked in height and brawn, he compensated for with speed. He dodged the silver blur of the blade, circled around, and dropped his own hand into his pocket. As the biker turned, looking to reacquire his prey, Red Jacket pulled out a can of mace. The biker's eyes bugged wide. He managed to get a hand up an instant before the chemical stream deployed.

Lou yanked open the restroom door, staggered out like a drunken bum, and collapsed a few feet outside.

A noxious cloud of pepper spray wafted into the restaurant. People at the nearest tables leaped from their seats, covering their noses and mouths. Lou managed to climb to his feet and stumble to the counter.

"Call 911!" he shouted at the waitress but could see through blurred vision that she was already on the phone. He sank heavily onto a stool as the bathroom door banged open and the man in the red jacket sprinted for the exit with the biker hot on his heels, bellowing and cursing.

The two men dashed across the parking lot to the highway where they faded into the shadows, swallowed by the featureless night.

TWO

"THERE HE GOES AGAIN," said Holly Bennett, topping off Lucas Stone's coffee cup. "Yankee Doodle Dandy."

"Who?" Stone saw that she was staring over his shoulder, out the window of the Birch Bark Diner and turned to follow her gaze. He spotted the hitchhiker on the other side of the road, thumb out, trying to catch a ride east. "You mean that guy?"

"Yeah, that guy," Holly confirmed. "Red jacket, white hat, and blue jeans. I call him Yankee Doodle Dandy. He hitchhikes out this way off and on."

"How often is 'off and on'?"

"I see him about once a month or so." Holly grinned and gave him a wink. "Don't be jealous. You're still my favorite bum."

"Glad to hear it." Stone smiled. "For a minute there, I thought I was gonna have to go arrest him."

Holly poured herself a half-cup of coffee and glanced around the empty diner. "Things really so boring in Garrison County that the sheriff has to go around slapping cuffs on hitchhikers? What's next, a crackdown on jaywalking? SWAT teams for litterbugs?"

"I like the way you think," Stone said, and they both laughed.

Lucas Stone had been living in Whisper Falls and patronizing the Birch Bark Diner for just over a year now. Haunted by the death of his daughter in Texas and subsequent divorce from his wife, Stone had left behind a violent past – his warrior days, he called it – and come to this small town in the Adirondack Mountains to remake himself.

Having graduated from seminary, he'd accepted a job here as pastor at Faith Bible Church. Not long after his arrival, he learned the county sheriff had raped and murdered a young girl, so Stone dragged him to the top of a mountain in the middle of a blizzard, stripped him naked, shot out his knees, and left him for the wild animals. Primal justice, damn straight.

He had then called in a few favors to be named the interim sheriff until the election in November. Now, as both pastor and sheriff, he was Whisper Falls' shepherd and sheepdog. It was a duality he was still adjusting to.

And despite following the Bible and wearing the badge, he still believed that sometimes justice was best served outside legal shackles.

He had also met Holly.

Stone studied her. Bright, a natural smart-ass, and easy on the eyes, Holly had quickly become his best friend. The mutual attraction to take things to the next level was there, lurking just beneath the surface, but by some unspoken agreement, they never reached for something more. They shared time, they shared laughs, they shared secrets. It was enough...for now.

"How's Lizzy?" he asked, taking a sip from his coffee cup.

"How do you think? She's a sixteen-year-old girl." Holly shook her head. "Nobody told me raising a teenage daughter would be this tough. I go back and forth between adoring her and wanting to strangle her."

"At least you've still got her," Stone said quietly, thinking about his daughter's grave in Texas.

They fell into a somber silence and Stone took a moment to glance out the window. The hitchhiker – Yankee Doodle Dandy – was gone, presumably having picked up a ride at some point in the past few minutes. Outside there was only cold, the crusted remains of the last snow dump, and a glaze of ice on the diner's window.

Stone returned his attention to Holly. "How have things been around here lately?"

"Pretty quiet." She shrugged. "They usually are in the winter. A few truckers. The local crowd. That's about it."

"There were some problems last night up toward Milford." Stone checked his watch. "I'm meeting the state police at the truck stop. Guess three guys got into a fight and one of them left on a stretcher. He's in intensive care and might not make it."

"My God…"

"The other two are still at large. State's criminal investigator wants me to look at the CCTV and see if I recognize anyone."

"Good ol' cop stuff," said Holly. "Probably makes you wish you had just stuck with your nice, safe church pulpit."

"The church gets its own share of the weird and the violent," Stone said grimly as he counted out some change. "That's why I've got Homer Pressfield coming to speak at tonight's service."

"Why does that name sound familiar?"

"You see him on the news sometimes. He's a preacher who happens to be an expert on political extremism."

Holly snapped her fingers. "That's right. I heard him on the radio last week. He was talking about some cult in Idaho near some lake. It was interesting."

"There's some real twisted mutations of Christianity out there." Stone shook his head in disgust as he stood up. "Take Christian Identitarians for example. They basically believe that Europeans are really God's chosen people."

Holly arched her eyebrows. "What does that make the Jews?"

"Satanic impostors." Stone found debates about politics, race, and extremism tedious, but keeping his flock informed was the right thing to do, given the current social climate. Homer Pressfield possessed the gift of passing along hard truths with a soft touch. He would give the congregation the information they needed without leaving them spooked.

"Sounds pretty heavy for a church meeting," Holly said.

Stone shrugged. "Jesus never said it would be easy. Only that it would be worth it." He touched the brim of his Stetson. "Gotta hit the road. I'll see you later."

Outside, Stone walked across the parking lot, breath fogging in the frigid air. They were a month past Christmas, but the really cold weather was only just now arriving in their neck of the woods. With the change in weather came a change in law enforcement activity. Stone and his small squad of deputies dealt with fewer vagrants and squatters during the cold months, but for some reason saw an uptick in thefts and break-ins.

Stone unlocked the door of his '78 Chevy Blazer. The truck had originally sported a two-tone red-and-white paint job, but he had painted it black and white when he became sheriff to match the department colors. He'd also installed a light bar and sirens. Sure, the sheriff had a tricked-out squad car assigned to him, but Stone preferred his Blazer.

He wasn't sure what job he preferred—sheriff or preacher. They both suited him, and he was unorthodox about both of them. He was a preacher who cussed, drank, and generally dismissed the so-called rules of organized religion. And he was a cop who was perfectly willing to break the law to deliver justice.

He started the Blazer, got the heat cranking, and called the station. Cade Valentine, his youngest deputy, answered on the second ring.

"Garrison County Sheriff's Department, Deputy Valentine speaking. How can I help you?"

"It's Stone. How are things at the shop?"

Stone sensed the young man's hesitation. Cade had worked for the previous sheriff, Grant Camden, and had despised the man. He hadn't seemed too broken up when Camden disappeared last December or when his bones had been discovered in the spring. But he still hadn't warmed up to his new boss, even though it had been over a year since Stone became sheriff.

"Everything's fine," Cade reported. "Got a call from the State Police letting us know the BCI detective is on his way to the truck stop. Other than that, it's the usual stuff. Missing dog out toward Silver Lake and a little fender bender out on Fletcher Farm Road."

"Anyone hurt?"

"Negative."

"Glad to hear it." Stone glanced at his watch. "Heading out to meet with BCI. I'll be back after lunch."

"Copy that."

Stone hung up, steered the Blazer out of the parking lot, and headed for the truck stop.

———

Founded in 1935, the Bureau of Criminal Investigation served as the plainclothes unit of the New York State Police. Far from just monitoring speed traps and handing out traffic tickets, the state patrol shouldered an active caseload of files ranging from money laundering and assault to special victims and counterterrorism. Stone had never worked with any BCI officers but had heard good things about the Bureau.

He parked the Blazer in the truck stop lot. A half dozen long-haulers had pulled up alongside the building and the lunch crowd had started to gather.

A tall man with a moustache and burly linebacker shoulders straining his trench coat was talking with a waitress at the cash register. Stone pegged him immediately as the BCI detective; he just looked the type. The BCI spotted the badge pinned to Stone's rancher coat and walked over.

"Jim Spencer, New York State Police." The guy offered his hand. "You must be Sheriff Stone."

"Guilty as charged."

"You heard about the incident here last night?"

"Just that three guys decided to throw down and one ended up in ICU."

"Happened around 9:30 PM." The detective flipped open a notepad and referred to his scribblings while he relayed the information. "Three men who the waitress identified as 'hanging around the place' for the past week all went into the bathroom at the same time. She got a bad feeling about it and the cook went in to have a look.

He got banged up pretty good but managed to give me a witness statement."

"Got some footage for me to look at?"

Spencer led Stone down the hallway to a back office. A New York state trooper sat at the desk, fiddling with the computer. Spencer said, "Okay, Tom. Go ahead and bring it up for us."

The trooper double-clicked on the icon that accessed the CCTV system. Stone dragged a chair over and sat as Spencer perched on the corner of the desk.

"We've got about seven minutes of footage isolated. I've sent copies to the lab to see about enhancing facial images we can insert into a state-wide BOLO. Meanwhile, we thought you might have some insight." Spencer nodded to the trooper. "Play the first clip."

The trooper clicked the mouse. Onscreen, a view of the entrance appeared, a man frozen in mid-step.

"This is our victim. Guy's name is Charles Hauser."

Another click of the mouse and the image of the man sprang to life. He walked through the camera shot and disappeared.

"That's the one in ICU? How's he doing?"

"Still unconscious." Spencer let out a frustrated sigh. "We're following up with his employer. Ring any bells for you?"

"Never seen him before."

"Okay." Spencer nodded to the trooper, who clicked the mouse again. "Here's our next guy. I'm guessing this'll get your attention."

The vestibule again, another frozen figure. When the trooper mouse-clicked and the figure started moving again, Stone let out a low whistle. "He's a member of the Children."

"Yeah." Spencer stared at the biker's image on the screen. "We've been monitoring some increased activity from the gang. Their visibility is definitely on the rise. I've got troopers reporting sightings all over the state, but particularly clustered up here in Troop B's area. So we're talking Franklin, Garrison, Essex, Clinton, Hamilton, and St. Lawrence counties."

Stone thought about telling Spencer that he knew what counties Troop B covered but decided to let it go. "Any idea what they're up to?" Stone leaned back in his chair. "Aside from the usual, I mean."

"You mean aside from the drugs, prostitution, gambling, and extortion? That's what's strange; we haven't had a bust on them in a while. They seem to be keeping their collective noses clean while spreading a net all over the state."

"Sure, they could just be staying out of trouble," Stone allowed. "Or they could be planning something big."

Spencer nodded. "We're thinking the latter."

Stone gestured at the screen. "Where's the third guy?"

"The entrance shot is obscured. We catch him in the next clip. Howard, run the third clip for me, would you?"

The mouse went click and another picture appeared on the monitor, this one a tight shot of the men's room door. Stone watched as the trucker entered. The biker followed less than ten seconds later.

"Third guy's already in there," Spencer said as the image of Lou the cook showed up on the screen. Stone watched him enter the bathroom. A minute later, he staggered out and collapsed just off camera.

"Here comes guy number three," Spencer said.

Stone leaned forward, eyes narrowed as he studied the screen. He saw the bathroom door fly open.

And then Yankee Doodle Dandy sprinted into the shot, pursued by the biker.

THREE

"YEAH, THAT'S HIM." Holly examined the CCTV printout before her on the kitchen table. "That's Yankee Doodle Dandy. I mean... I *think* it is..."

Stone gave her a look. "You think?"

"It looks like him. Clothes, build, things like that. I just never got a close-up of his face before. But yeah, it sure does look like him."

Holly had finished her shift at 2:00 PM and met Stone back at her place. Over the past year, they had developed the kind of easygoing friendship in which dropping by each other's homes was normal. Stone spent enough time at Holly's that she kept a bottle of Jack Daniels and a six-pack of Coke on hand for him. But this afternoon he opted for coffee instead of whiskey while she indulged in an after-work glass of wine.

"Tell me what you remember about this guy." Stone tapped the photo of Yankee Doodle. "When was the first time you saw him?"

"Not sure." Holly traced the rim of her glass with a fingertip. "He's such a common sight that he just started to blend in. Like wallpaper, you know?"

"Just do your best."

She gave it some thought. "Must have been last spring. I remember the weather was still chilly, but it wasn't winter anymore. Probably right around the time those hikers found Sheriff Camden's body up by the waterfall."

Stone kept his expression neutral. He had shared a lot of secrets with Holly, but he had never told her about his part in Camden's disappearance. Some things were best left between him, God, and the devil.

"So probably around April or so," she continued. "That jacket really catches your eye. Bright red and big. And there he was, hitchhiking across the road from the diner. After that, every time I saw the jacket, I knew it was him."

"You said about once a month or so, right?"

"At least once a month. Sometimes more."

"And he always wore the same jacket?"

"Same jacket. Same jeans. Same...hey, are you thinking—?"

"I'm thinking that's a damn heavy jacket to wear in the summer."

Holly's eyes widened. "Jeez, why didn't I notice that? But now that you mention it, yes. Always wearing that red jacket, always wearing the white hat, always wearing those blue jeans."

"Maybe he's homeless," Stone said. "Lots of homeless guys wear the same clothes all the time."

"For months and months? Hell, Luke, the guy's hitch-hiked in front of the diner probably eighteen, nineteen times, always wearing those exact same clothes."

"It's strange, I'll give you that," Stone said.

The thumping of footsteps on the three-season porch and the sound of the front door opening alerted them that Lizzy, Holly's daughter, was home from school.

"Hi, Mom." Lizzy glided into the kitchen, dumped her backpack on the floor, and yanked open the refrigerator door. "Hey, Luke." Her voice was muffled by the interior of the fridge as she foraged for food.

"How was school?" Holly asked as Lizzy grabbed a bag of corn chips and sat down at the table with a bowl of guacamole she had scrounged from the refrigerator.

She was a pretty-faced kid with olive-toned skin, large eyes, and prominent cheekbones, and she liked to experiment with her looks and style. She had recently dyed the purple streaks in her hair so that it was all black and then chopped it short. Stone thought she looked like Joan Jett, then wondered if someone as young as Lizzy even knew who Joan Jett was.

"It was fine." Lizzy glanced at the CCTV pictures. "Hey, that's Yankee Doodle," she said.

"You've seen him too?" Stone asked.

"Yep." Lizzy bit into a chip, then chewed and talked at the same time. "I worked a few shifts last summer with Mom over at the Birch Bark. Mom pointed him out and told me his nickname."

"Wearing the same red jacket?"

"Yeah. Always." She pointed at another printout. "How come you have a picture of a biker?"

Stone felt a surge of alarm. "How do you know about the Children?"

Lizzy made a face. "Stanley's mom is dating one."

"Stanley is in Lizzy's art class," Holly explained.

"Sometimes he comes by on his bike to give Stanley a lift after school." Lizzy dipped a chip. "Guy looks like a grizzly bear."

"He look anything like this guy?" Stone pointed at the picture.

"I can't tell," Lizzy said. "They all look the same."

They look all the same…

Something about that phrase resonated with Stone, banging around in his skull like an odd echo. He was still thinking about it when his cell phone rang.

"This is Stone."

"Sheriff, it's Valentine." The deputy sounded out of breath. "We've got a vehicular murder."

"A what?"

"You heard me, sheriff. A vehicular murder. It's when someone uses a vehicle to kill somebody."

"I know what it means, deputy."

"I've got a body splattered like roadkill and one suspect in custody. Just past Milford, right before the I-87 on-ramp."

"On my way," Stone said. He hung up.

"What's going on?" Holly asked.

"Trouble," Stone replied. "Gotta go."

FOUR

STONE COULD SEE the mess on the road even from a distance. Approaching the cloverleaf where the two lanes of Route 374 looped onto Interstate 87—the Northway, as it was commonly called—he saw a stationary eighteen-wheeler parked on the shoulder. The left lane remained open, a state trooper using a glow stick to direct the slow-crawling traffic around the crime scene. Lights flashed from the strategically parked police cars as Stone pulled up behind the nearest one. His own light bar pulsed red and blue.

Cade Valentine approached as Stone exited the Blazer. "Hey, sheriff." The deputy spoke softly, clearly a bit shaken up. "It's real ugly."

"What have we got?" Stone headed toward the scene, Valentine trailing.

"Trucker killed a biker," the deputy replied. "That's the long and the short of it, according to eyewitnesses and even the trucker himself, I guess, since he's not denying anything. Looks like he just ran his truck right up behind the guy's motorcycle and..." Valentine punched his fist into his palm to mimic the sound of a hard impact.

Just short of the I-87 on-ramp, Stone spotted a Milford city worker hosing down a long red streak on the pavement that ran for two hundred yards beyond the mangled Harley that laid twisted on the road like a crushed metal insect.

"The truck rammed the bike from behind." Valentine nodded toward the blackened nose of the eighteen-wheeler. "Smashed it flat and scraped the biker all over the road. I've got the trucker in the back of my cruiser."

"Where's the body?" Stone asked.

"Over here." Valentine led him to an ambulance parked behind the truck, its back door open to expose a draped form on a gurney.

Stone gestured at the paramedic. "Let's have a look."

The man leaned forward, grabbed the blanket, and hesitated. "It's not pretty," he warned.

"Dead bodies usually aren't," Stone said grimly. "Show me."

The paramedic drew back the blanket. There wasn't much left that was recognizably human. Most of the biker's distinguishing features were mangled, his face scrubbed off by the concrete. His clothes were shredded but Stone still recognized the vest. The road-killed corpse had been part of a gang, out on a ride and flying his colors when he got smacked by a semi.

"He's one of the Children," Stone commented.

"Sure looks that way," Valentine replied. "I chased off a reporter right after I got here. I don't think he saw anything, but you never know."

"Not a big deal either way." Stone moved away from the ambulance. "The Children will figure it out soon enough, if they haven't already, and when they do, they'll want blood." *And I'm half-tempted to let them have it,* Stone thought silently. Aloud he continued, "We'll put our suspect in protective custody. Got a rundown on him?"

"His name is Roger Dorey. Licensed air-break operator employed by Cardine Trucking in Milford. Small-time criminal record. One drunk and disorderly, one assault, a few traffic tickets, that sort of thing."

"He have anything to say for himself?"

"Nothing." Valentine nodded toward his parked cruiser, the red-and-blues flashing as the suspect sat in the back cage. "He's flat-out refused to answer any questions about what happened. Mind you, he's got plenty of opinions about everything else…"

"Let me talk to him." Stone leaned against the trunk of Valentine's cruiser and waited.

The young deputy opened the back door and helped the trucker, hands cuffed behind his back, exit the car. He marched Dorey to the rear of the Crown Vic and presented him to Stone.

"Thanks, Cade. I'll take it from here."

"He's all yours." Valentine wandered off to chat with the paramedic, leaving the trucker alone with the sheriff.

Stone studied the man. Dorey had one of those unfortunate fleshy faces that looked permanently immature despite the five o'clock shadow and graying hair. He glared at Stone, the stereotypical middle-aged trucker with a beer gut and an attitude. Stone had met his fair share along the way.

"I'm Sheriff Stone." Stone folded his arms. "Tell me what happened here."

"You got eyes," Dorey snapped. "Open 'em up and take a look for yourself."

"I did," Stone replied. "And you know what I'm thinking?"

"Spell it out for me, copper."

"I'm thinking twenty to life." Stone allowed his

honey-colored eyes, flat and hard, to settle on the man. "We've got enough physical evidence and eyewitnesses to prove that you intentionally rammed the victim's motorcycle and dragged him down the road until he was dead." Stone paused for effect, then rasped, "That's murder one, asshole."

Dorey hawked up some phlegm, spat on the ground between Stone's boots, and growled, "That's his tough luck."

"Luck is something you're going to be shit-outta if you don't cooperate. Tell me why you killed him."

Dorey smiled smugly. Stone knew the look. Dorey was a man harboring secrets, the reasons, and motives for what he had done. And he wanted Stone to know that he didn't have a hope in hell of dragging it out of him.

Stone gave it a shot anyway. "Listen, man, cooperating with us really is the best way to—"

"Kiss my ass! I don't cooperate with dumbass cops. You're all a bunch of clowns, you know that? Worse than useless. A bunch of pathetic bullies and cowards who hide behind their guns and badges. But you're no different from any other goddamned gang. I got more respect for the hood rats and wetbacks that form their own crews. At least they don't pretend to be looking out for motherfucking *strangers*!"

Stone's eyes narrowed. "What strangers are you talking about?"

"Outsiders. Foreigners. People who don't belong, dammit! All that matters is taking care of your own. But do-gooder cowboy cops like you make a big deal about protecting other people's 'rights.' What the hell do you know about what's right?"

"I know it's not right to turn someone into roadkill. For God's sake, he looks like somebody took a belt sander to him."

"I hope the son of a bitch suffered. I hope he was alive long enough to feel his skin getting peeled off."

Stone clenched his jaw and seriously considered driving a fist into the trucker's flabby gut. The racist bastard deserved to be knocked to the ground and get the crap kicked out of him until he was nothing but a busted-up mess of blood and bile. But right now was not the time and right here was not the place.

"You got a lawyer?" Stone asked.

"Sure do. Called him before the body even stopped twitching."

"Good." Stone tossed Dorey back in the cruiser with way more roughness than necessary and slammed the door shut. "You're gonna need him."

FIVE

STONE HEADED HOME for a shower and a change of clothes. It had been a long day and it wasn't over yet. He was scheduled to meet Pastor Pressfield at the church in a few hours to set up for tonight's service and he still wanted a crack at Dorey while the shock of arrest was fresh. In his experience, this was when suspects were the most pliable.

An hour or two behind bars might loosen his tongue and get him to drop the tough-guy act, Stone thought as he steered the Blazer off the main road and down the tree-lined, 500-foot driveway to the parsonage. Snow clung to the branches of the pines like pristine puffs of cotton candy while a crust of ice had formed in the gravel potholes he kept neglecting to fill in.

Years back, long before Stone's arrival in town, a wealthy parishioner had donated the 30-acre parcel of land to Faith Bible Church. The congregation had pulled together enough money through donations and fundraisers to build a new parsonage, an 1,800 square foot, single-story ranch house that Stone now called home. Set back from the road, surrounded by woods, and with no nearby neighbors, the place was a private oasis of peace for him.

Stone pulled up in front of the three-car garage and killed the engine. He lingered in the driver's seat, listening to the metallic tick of the motor as it started to cool down, savoring the tranquility of his home.

It hadn't always been this way. Last year a group of renegade survivalists had shot up the house. The insurance paid for the damage, but the survivalists paid with their lives. Not because they wrecked his home, but because in the aftermath, they threatened Holly and Lizzy. It had been too much for Stone to take. The warrior within him had been resurrected.

Target people he cared about and Stone would rain hellfire down on your head without mercy, make no mistake. That might not be the godliest approach for a preacher, but Stone was learning to live with his Jekyll and Hyde syndrome, the duality of his nature, the sacred and the savage somehow finding a way to coexist.

After a time, he went inside. Kicking off his boots and leaving his Stetson and rancher's coat in the mudroom, Stone padded to the bedroom. His dog Max – a scar-faced Shottie – lolled on the bed, looking like the laziest mutt to ever be rescued from a shelter.

Stone paused to scratch the dog's head. "You know, other dogs greet their owners at the door when they get home."

Max gave him a look that seemed to say, *If you wanted a normal dog, you shouldn't have picked me.*

Stone rolled the Shottie over for a quick belly rub, then stripped and stepped into the shower.

The water pressure from the twin nozzles felt great as he stood beneath the pulsing streams of hot water. Closing his eyes, Stone emptied his mind and just let the pounding warmth wash over him. Between his pastoral responsibilities and his sheriff duties, he stayed incredibly busy, so sometimes these stolen moments were the only snippets of pleasure he could snatch from the controlled chaos of his life.

He imagined himself standing under a waterfall, the hiss and splash of water loud enough to drown out all other noise.

Except...

His eyes snapped open.

He felt, rather than heard, a menacing rumble.

His senses immediately went on high alert. He cranked the handle to turn off the water and listened intently.

There it was again.

Not a sound, exactly. More like the echo of a sound. And the air still felt like it was trembling. Stone toweled off, pulled on his jeans, and tugged his Glock 21 pistol from its holster.

Moving silently on bare feet, he slipped up the hall, through the kitchen, and into the spare bedroom at the front of the house. Max followed, silent as well; the dog never made a sound. Stone parted the blinds that covered the large window. Hanging in the air above the driveway was a dissipating cloud of gray exhaust smoke.

Shirtless but ignoring the cold, Stone went to the front door and stepped outside. The smell of spent fuel polluted the fresh mountain air. He crouched down and examined the gravel.

Stone had received some tracker training during his warrior days, but nothing that qualified him as an expert. He'd once worked with a half-Apache operator who could track a centipede across twenty miles of sunbaked rock, but that was not a gift Stone possessed. But he didn't need much expertise to figure out what had happened here.

Fresh tracks, two sets. Not a car but a pair of motorcycles, big ones, judging from the depth of the tracks. Something cold snaked into his guts as Stone deduced that two Harleys from the Children had followed him home and reconnoitered his place while he showered. The vibrating rumble he had heard was the bikes' notorious and obnoxiously loud engines. Clearly the bikers had not cared if he knew they were there. Hell, maybe they *wanted* him to know they were there.

Stone stepped back into the house and locked the door behind him.

SIX

"WHERE'S DOREY?"

"I stuck him in interview room two. But…"

"What is it, Cade?"

Valentine fidgeted. "He's lawyered up. He hired—"

"Ah, Sheriff Stone, there you are!"

At the sound of that voice, Stone closed his eyes and gritted his teeth.

Scott Slidell, attorney-at-law and Whisper Falls' busiest ambulance chaser, glided into the room. With his breezy blond pompadour and California frat boy good looks, Slidell could have easily become an actor. And in a way, he had; he was well-known for his often outrageous courtroom theatrics and bullying cross-examinations.

Slidell was the lawyer of choice for Garrison County's scumbags and bottom feeders, a reputation he carefully cultivated. Despite the gold cuff links and tailored suits, Slidell often took cases for barter or pro-bono rates – anything to maintain a healthy caseload representing the county's less-savory citizens.

"Counselor. So good to see you again." The sarcasm practically oozed between Stone's clenched teeth, but he figured it was better than punching the defense attorney in the chops, which is what he really wanted to do.

"Well, look at you, sheriff. You seem to have worked on your manners where interacting with your fellow laborers in the vineyard of American justice is concerned. And that's a good thing, because law enforcement must be held to a higher standard than your average citizen, don't you agree? Of course you do! I'm sure you aspire—"

"Shut up, Slidell."

The lawyer just kept on rolling. "—aspire to the highest levels of professionalism. Take, for example, my client, Mr. Dorey. Since your staff failed to provide my client with adequate nourishment for his physical needs, I must insist he be seen by a medical professional immediately."

"What are you talking about?"

"Mr. Dorey has diabetes." Slidell shot Valentine a disgusted look. "By refusing to feed him properly, your deputy has placed my client's life in jeopardy."

Stone glanced over at Cade.

"We fed him, sheriff." Stone could tell Valentine was struggling to keep his composure under Slidell's withering assault. "The usual. Ham sub from the deli, bag of chips, apple, carton of milk."

"That's not enough for a man with Mr. Dorey's extraordinary medical condition." Slidell folded his arms dramatically. "I insist that you release him at once."

"Cade, did Dorey tell you about his 'extraordinary medical condition' during processing?" Stone asked.

"Negative," Valentine replied.

"There you have it." Stone spread his hands. "We ask every suspect we bring in if they have any medical issues we need to know about. Since your client decided to keep his mouth shut, we can't be held liable. So unless he's flopping around on the floor having a diabetic crash, we'll keep him here for now."

"An unwise decision, Sheriff Stone." Slidell shook his head dramatically. "And, I daresay, one that might very well return to haunt you down the road. But as it happens, Mr. Dorey is well enough to speak to you, so I shall grant you permission."

"I don't need your permission," Stone growled. "Your client deliberately rammed a biker and smeared him all over the road."

"Correction – he *appears* to have deliberately rammed a motorcyclist. The level of premeditation has yet to be established."

"You keep telling yourself that." Stone brushed past the attorney and entered the windowless interview room.

Dorey sat with his head bowed and the remains of his jailhouse lunch scattered on the table in front of him. Mounted on a bracket in the corner was a CCTV camera that fed directly into the observation room next door.

"How are you, Mr. Dorey?" Slidell patted the trucker on the shoulder. "Feeling better since you received some nourishment?"

"I'm fine." Dorey lobbed a look at Stone. "Other than my mistreatment by the sheriff, of course."

"Cut the crap." Stone yanked out a chair, spun it around, and swung a leg over to sit with his arms resting on the back. Slidell took a seat beside the trucker. "Just tell me why you killed that biker."

"Don't answer that," Slidell said to Dorey, then flashed a gleaming smile at Stone. "Nice try, sheriff, but you should know better than to try and bully a confession out of my client."

"This isn't me being a bully. This is me trying to cut through the bullshit." Stone reached into his jacket pocket, unfolded a sheet of paper, and placed it before Dorey. "You know him?"

The shock of recognition crossed Dorey's face as he examined the image of Charles Hauser, pulled from the CCTV footage. Stone had decided not to lead with the crime scene photos that showed Hauser beaten unconscious, but he was willing to bet Dorey knew all about it. News traveled fast among the trucking network.

Slidell glanced at the picture. "Sheriff Stone, I don't know where you're going with this, but—"

Stone kept his gaze fixed on the trucker and put some ice in his voice. "Answer the question, Dorey."

"Wait just one minute, sheriff..." Slidell started to protest.

"I'm not waiting for shit," Stone rasped. "Answer me, Dorey. Right now."

Slidell seemed thrown off balance by Stone's harsh tone, unsure of what to say. Dorey fidgeted, glanced at the picture again, and then looked up at Stone.

"Yeah, I know him. That's Charlie."

"You guys both work for Cardine Trucking over in Milford, right?"

Dorey nodded.

"You aware that Hauser is in ICU after getting a beat down at the truck stop last night?"

"Yeah, I'm aware." Dorey's eyes blazed with anger. "That goddamn animal broke his skull!"

"Stay calm, Mr. Dorey. It's in your best interest," Slidell advised, feebly trying to rein in the trucker's rage, well aware that Dorey might say something in the heat of the moment that could derail his defense when he got to court.

"Stay calm? Fuck that! Charlie's not ever gonna be the same!" Dorey's fury practically spilled from his pores. "Even if he lives, he'll never drive a truck again. Hell, he might not even be able to feed himself or wipe his own ass when this is done!"

"And you blame the Children for that?" Stone asked.

"You're damn right I do!"

"Enough!" Slidell shot to his feet and glared at Stone. "I'm ending this interview right now. My client is starving, suffering from medical distress, accused of a crime he didn't commit, and now you've driven him into a rage with your spurious questioning. I demand you release him at once!" Slidell checked his Rolex. "Time's up, anyway. Let's go, Mr. Dorey."

"Not so fast," said Stone.

Slidell looked impatient. "You can't hold him any longer."

"Yes, we can, and you know it. Don't worry, we'll hit him with charges before our time runs out."

"*What* charges?" Slidell demanded.

"Conspiracy to commit murder," Stone replied. "Don't worry, you'll be able to visit your client, but right now your time is up. Say goodbye and hit the road."

It wasn't very preacher-like, but Stone enjoyed the fuming look on Slidell's face as the defense attorney gathered his things. He clearly didn't like being told what to do. And the dangerous glint in the lawyer's eye let Stone know that the man was taking it personal.

"When I'm finished making your life miserable, Sheriff Stone, you'll be fortunate if you can obtain employment as a school crossing guard," Slidell hissed.

"Was it something I said?" Stone drawled.

The attorney pointed at Dorey. "First I will have justice for this falsely-arrested man." The finger switched over to Stone. "And then I will have my revenge. See you in court, cowboy."

SEVEN

DUSK HAD FALLEN like a spreading bruise and Stone had an hour or so to kill before Homer Pressfield was scheduled to arrive for his presentation. He noticed a motorcycle in his rear-view mirror as he mulled over his game plan for making the murder charge stick to Dorey.

Hauser and Dorey both worked for Cardine Trucking. He needed to isolate and interview their co-workers. He would bet dollars to dimes that at least one of them would crack and admit to workplace conversations about getting payback on the Children, and that would be more than enough for Stone to work with.

He glanced at the mirror again.

The biker was still on his tail.

Enough of this shit.

Time to stop playing cat-and-mouse games with the Children and start getting some answers.

He had some time to spare. He turned down a little-used road just past a Stewart's convenience store. The Harley followed, staying back but clearly sticking to his six.

Stone had changed into a clean shirt and blazer in

preparation for tonight's church service, leaving his Glock at home. But like any cop, he had an off-duty carry. His Colt Cobra .38 snub-nosed revolver rode in the right pocket of his blazer, all six cylinders bristling with hollow points.

The biker was probably packing firepower, too, but Stone didn't care. He was more comfortable with violent confrontations than he sometimes cared to admit. Besides, if everything went according to plan, he wouldn't even need the Colt.

He followed the road out past the western edge of town to the old grain elevator and loading platform that had once serviced the now-defunct rail line. Thirty years ago, trains had run through the outskirts of Whisper Falls and stopped to load up on feed for livestock. But now the grain elevator sat rusted in the unforgiving elements, a relic of a forgotten time brooding among the cluster of neglected brick buildings slowly falling apart with each passing season. The largest eyesore was a multi-story warehouse squatting next to the grain silo.

Stone checked to make sure the bike was still trailing him, then whipped the Blazer between two buildings. A wide bay door opened onto the dark interior of the warehouse. He drove inside, exited the truck, grabbed a crowbar from the assortment of tools he kept in the back, and ran back to the edge of the building.

He could hear the rumble of the Harley as it slowed, chugging down a gear as the biker approached the turn between the two buildings cautiously. Stone flexed his fingers around the crowbar, getting a good grip, waiting to strike.

The engine revved as the Harley sped up slightly in order to stay balanced. The front wheel came into view...

Stone raised the crowbar like a Louisville Slugger, wound up like Babe Ruth getting ready to knock it out of the park, and stepped forward as the biker turned the corner.

He swung the crowbar at chest level. But he hadn't counted on the tall mirrors mounted on each side of the bike's handlebars. Rather than slam into the biker and knock him off the motorcycle, the crowbar connected with one of the mirror stands.

Metal bent and glass shattered. The biker threw up a hand and twisted away from the spray of fragments. The handlebars skewed to the side and the Harley toppled over.

The biker threw himself off before his leg got crushed beneath the falling machine. He hit the ground, rolled, and came up with a chain in his fist.

Stone leaped over the still-rumbling Harley and swung the crowbar again. For a beefy, bearded biker hauling around a beer gut, the biker proved surprisingly fast on his feet. He dodged out of range just quick enough to avoid impact. Stone silently cursed his swing-and-a-miss. He should have just used the damn gun.

The biker took his shot, and the chain gave him a serious reach advantage. Stone saw it coming, ducked to the side, and narrowly missed getting a bunch of iron links upside the head. Had it landed, he knew it would have split his scalp, knocked him out, or possibly even cracked open his skull.

Hell with this.

He dropped the crowbar and drew the Colt .38 from his pocket as the biker hauled the chain back again like a metal scourge.

"Drop it!" Stone snarled.

The chain whipped out before he got the gun on target, the links coiling around his right wrist like an attacking python. The blow knocked the pistol out of his hand and sent pain radiating up his arm.

The biker yanked on the chain, controlling Stone like a lassoed steer. Stone found himself jerked off his feet and thrown against the wall of the building. He managed to bring his free arm up to break the force of the pile drive, but he still banged his head off the bricks before crashing to the ground.

Dazed by the blow, Stone managed to roll up onto all fours as the chain around his wrist went slack. As he shook his head to clear away the dazzling starbursts ricocheting inside his skull and the blood dripping into his eye, he heard his assailant fire up the Harley. By the time Stone regained his feet, the bike and its rider had disappeared into the dusk.

EIGHT

"LUKE, WHAT HAPPENED?"

Stone was surprised to find Holly and Lizzy waiting for him at the church when he arrived. They were not members of the Faith Bible congregation but had apparently decided to attend tonight's presentation by Homer Pressfield.

Stone ignored her question and said, "You're early. Service doesn't start for another hour."

Holly shrugged. "We were just sitting around the house doing nothing, so we figured we'd head over here and see if you needed help with anything before the service." Her eyes narrowed. "Now stop dodging my question. What happened to you?"

Stone had managed to camouflage the slight limp he'd acquired since getting banged around by the biker. But the torn sleeve of his blazer, swollen right wrist, and the gash above his left eye were harder to conceal. He did, however, manage to hide his injured pride. Getting dumped in the dirt by a biker stung.

"Traffic stop," he deadpanned as he dug for his keys.

Holly rolled her eyes. "Traffic stop, my ass."

Stone led them through the church to his office. He fetched the first-aid kit and took it with him into the bathroom. He found some Tylenol in the medicine cabinet behind the mirror and dry-swallowed three tablets. Then he turned on the taps and spoke over the sound of running water.

"We're having trouble with the Children." Stone winced at the shiner covering his left eye. "One of them followed me on the way over here, so I stopped to deal with him. Looks like a couple of them checked out my place earlier today too."

Lizzy said, "You got your ass kicked? Thought that never happened."

Stone could hear the friendly smirk in her voice. God, he really liked this kid. "Nobody wins all the time," he said.

"Next time just shoot the guy," Lizzy suggested.

"Lizzy." Holly's voice held a warning note.

"I'm just saying."

"Well, don't."

"Fine. I'll be outside, getting some fresh air from all the mothering going on in here."

Stone adjusted the taps and lathered up his hands. "Be a good idea for you guys to be extra careful the next couple of days." He scrubbed the blood off his head wound and applied some disinfectant, then flexed his fingers. Still some pain there but he could pull a trigger if he had to. He peered out the bathroom door and looked at Holly. "Keep that gun of yours handy."

She nodded her understanding.

Holly had seen her own share of trouble in life. She and Lizzy had relocated to Whisper Falls under the auspices of the Federal Witness Protection Program. Stone admired the way his friend had worked to start over with a new, safer life for her daughter, far away from the nasty hoodlum she had testified against – her ex-husband, who happened to be a Vegas mob boss. Thanks to Holly, he was now rotting at a federal prison in California.

Stone knew there was nothing she wouldn't do to protect Lizzy. Just last year she had gunned down a man in her living room who had made the fatal mistake of thinking they were easy prey. If the Children were foolish enough to mess with Holly, they might find themselves looking for a bulk discount on cheap coffins.

"Here." Holly held out a jacket from his office closet as he came out of the bathroom. "Found this replacement for you."

"Thanks."

Lizzy popped back into the office. "Luke, there's some guy out here asking for you."

Stone donned the fresh jacket and went to greet Homer Pressfield. Shaking hands, Stone was amused to see his fellow pastor gaping at his black eye.

"Good Lord!" Pressfield exclaimed. "Is this a church or a fight club?"

"You should see the other guy," Stone said with a crooked grin. "I told him to tithe at least ten percent."

———

Homer Pressfield was a hale, stocky, sixty-five-year-old man who carried a little extra weight around his middle and suffered from thinning hair on top. But that failed to dim his smile or the merry sparkle in his eye. He was a gifted speaker who seemed to genuinely connect with his audience. If Stone had any doubts about the man's ability to hold his congregation's attention, they dispelled quickly.

"One of the things that make being a Christian so

much fun," Pressfield said, "is being part of a club." He grinned as the small congregation chuckled. "A sense of belonging has a powerful appeal and there are elements of our faith that call to a very lonesome part of us. Mostly we hope that fellowship is positive, but it isn't always so. Think of David Koresh or Jim Jones and the People's Temple in Guyana. Those misguided pastors – and I use that term loosely – spoke of apocalyptic matters, drew disillusioned and disaffected people into a tight-knit community, and brought hundreds to death and ruin."

He paused for a moment and let his bright, warm gaze linger on the people listening intently to him before he continued.

"In my work, I study political extremism through a Christian lens. That means I have to study and learn about some very unpleasant things, but we cannot bury our heads in the sand when it comes to evil. In order to defeat our enemy, we must know our enemy. These are dangerous people engaged in serious crimes."

Pressfield touched a key on the laptop on the lectern. A photo appeared on the large screen behind him. The image showed a dozen or so people, all dressed in black, holding automatic weapons. They posed in front of a wall spray-painted with a red symbol that was blatantly evil and ugly. Something inside Stone recoiled at the sight, and he could tell the congregation felt it too.

"This is arguably the most dangerous White Nationalist group in the country right now." Pressfield paused for emphasis. "No faction is more feared than The Remnant."

The next slide revealed a close-up of the red symbol.

"The Remnant calls this The Sickle. As you can see, it incorporates a crucifix while swastikas adorn the top and the ends of both arms. It's surrounded by an inverted pentagram star, called a 'Baphomet,' and everything is enclosed within a trapezoid. The Remnant believe it projects actual spiritual power." Pressfield let everyone get a good, long look at the symbol, then tapped a button on the laptop and the picture faded into a photograph of a peaceful country forest. "Ah, that's much better."

Several members of the congregation smiled, clearly relieved not to have The Sickle thrust in their face any longer.

"The Remnant is an unusual group," Pressfield said. "It's primarily composed of ex- and AWOL members of the Canadian and US armed forces. For some reason, The Remnant appeals to soldier types, and that makes them even more dangerous than your typical white supremacy group."

Pressfield leaned forward, his solemn voice filling every corner of the sanctuary. "They call themselves a church. They claim to be Christian. Their theology is a Molotov cocktail of traditional Christian Identity beliefs and the sick philosophy of Charles Manson. Like Jim Jones and David Koresh before them, they preach an apocalypse gospel. But unlike those men, The Remnant do not believe they will be bystanders to the apocalypse. They believe they will actually help usher it in."

———

After the service ended, Stone, Holly, and Lizzy sat around the kitchen table at the parsonage. Max laid on his bed over by the couch, pretending to be aloof but actually keeping a close eye on them in case somebody had some food.

"That Pressfield guy seemed cool enough," Lizzy said. "But all the stuff he talked about was pretty creepy."

"I don't understand the biblical aspects," Holly

confessed. She leaned over and nudged Stone with her elbow. "Care to explain, preacher?"

"Sure. Right after I fix myself a drink."

"I'll get it. You talk." Holly stood up and headed for the kitchen. "Jack and Coke, lots of ice, easy on the Jack?" she asked, as if she hadn't made it for him dozens of times before.

"That sounds like a winner," Stone replied.

"Make it two," Lizzy chimed in. "No Coke in mine."

"Nice try, kiddo." Holly got to work making the drink while Stone got to explaining.

"There are figures associated with the Apocalypse called the Four Horsemen. In the Bible, each one rides a horse of a different color. The Remnant has decided those colors correspond to the different races."

"Isn't that what Manson was all about?" asked Lizzy.

"Charles Manson believed in a race war," Holly replied.

Stone looked at her in surprise.

She shrugged. "I went through a phase." She brought over his drink and sat back down. "I was fascinated with the Manson Family and studied what they were all about."

"Look at Mom, going all dark and wicked," Lizzy teased.

Holly rolled her eyes, ignored the comment, and continued, "Charlie talked about something he called 'Helter Skelter,' named after a song by the Beatles. It was his code name for a race war in America. Blacks against whites. He believed there would be death on a massive scale."

"So do The Remnant," said Stone. "Difference between them and Manson is that they see themselves as one of the Horsemen. They see it as their job to kick off the race war and jumpstart the Apocalypse."

"So they go around murdering people," Lizzy said.

"Yeah." Stone swirled his Jack and Coke, making the ice cubes clink against the glass. "They're basically Nazis with itchy trigger fingers."

"Sounds like a great bunch of guys," Holly muttered.

Stone started to raise his glass to take a drink when his cell phone rang. He glanced at the caller ID and saw that it was Deputy Valentine. He tapped the screen to accept the call. "This is Stone."

"Sheriff, it's Cade." The deputy rarely used his last name because he thought it sounded girly. "I'm out at the Birch Bark Diner. We've got another body on our hands."

———

This has got to be the longest day of my life, Stone thought.

A lot had happened since his morning coffee with Holly at the Birch Bark and their chat about Yankee Doodle Dandy. That seemed like an eternity ago. Right now, Stone wanted nothing more than to go home and crawl into bed. But the day wasn't done with him yet and duty called.

Emergency lights strobed the night as he pulled up to the gaggle of police cars – and one ambulance – parked on the shoulder of the road just past the diner. He parked the Blazer and walked across the road where Valentine waited for him, looking every bit as exhausted as he felt.

"Hey, sheriff," the deputy greeted wearily. "Body's over here."

Stone followed him to the shallow ditch alongside the road. In springtime, it would be filled with runoff, but this time of year it was stuffed with a foot of snow. A section of the ditch was covered by a tarp.

"A motorist spotted him and gave us a call," Valentine said as he leaned over and pulled back the tarp.

Stone felt a jolt of recognition.

"We took some pictures, but I haven't checked him for ID yet," the deputy continued. "But one thing we do know about him is that he's a patriotic son of a bitch."

Stone stared down at the red jacket, white cap, and blue jeans. "Yeah," he said quietly. "He's a real Yankee Doodle Dandy."

NINE

STONE SLEPT like a corpse and if he dreamed of dead men, he didn't remember it. He woke up feeling mostly refreshed and a quick shower and a cup of coffee took care of the rest.

Max shambled into the kitchen.

"Want some breakfast, buddy?" Stone set his empty coffee mug in the sink and rubbed the top of the Shottie's scarred head, then dumped some food into his dish. As he watched Max wolf it down, he listened to his voice-mail messages.

The first, from the coroner's office, had been left at 3:00 AM and contained an initial report on the subject and cause of death. The man's name was Andrew Irwin, twenty-one years of age, according to the United States Army ID in his pocket. The cause of death was massive blunt force trauma to the body.

"In other words, sheriff," the coroner said, "the extensive damage to bones and internal organs indicates that he was killed when he got struck by a vehicle."

Could just be an accidental death, Stone thought. A regular old hit-and-run. But given Yankee Doodle

Dandy's connection to the events at the truck stop, Stone seriously doubted it. More than likely, the "massive blunt force trauma" had been generated by 900 pounds of Harley steel hurling into Andrew Irwin's body.

Stone had a pretty good idea where his investigation would take him next.

———

"The Children?" Holly leaned across the counter and topped off Stone's coffee. "You think they're involved in this?"

"I'd say it's a good possibility," Stone replied.

"You think they're mixed up with those neo-Nazis? The Remnant?"

"Hard to say. Maybe. It's not like you see a lot of black guys in biker gangs."

"Good point." Holly scuttled off to deliver a plate of pancakes to a waiting customer. When she got back, she said, "I know the Children are an offshoot of another gang. The Huns, I think. For the most part, they stay out of Whisper Falls, other than to pass through. You know Blaine's Billiards?"

Stone nodded. The pool hall was fifteen miles up the road, about halfway between Whisper Falls and Milford.

"That's their clubhouse," Holly said.

"How do you know that?"

"Lizzy. That's the buzz on the high school grapevine, anyway. You think Griz knows everything that goes on in this town? He ain't got nothing on a bunch of gossiping teenage girls."

Stone said thanks, drained his coffee, and hit the road. It was time to pay the Children a visit.

———

Was there a link between the Children and The Remnant? Stone pondered the possibility as he followed Route 3 out of town, heading east.

He needed answers. Unfortunately, Dorey was keeping his mouth shut on Slidell's advice. Hauser was still unconscious in ICU. Yankee Doodle Dandy, a.k.a. Andrew Irwin, was bagged and tagged on a mortuary slab. The only ones left who could still talk were the Children.

There was obviously bad blood between the Children and the Cardine truckers. Stone knew that if he didn't get to the bottom of that conflict, Garrison County could be looking at a full-blown gang war playing out on the rural highways, with bikers and truckers cranking up the body count on a daily basis.

Stone had witnessed firsthand the level of carnage they could inflict. During his warrior days, he had been on assignment in a small South American republic where two major gangs waged a street war over control of the narcotics trade. The feud had escalated rapidly and consumed the capitol. The collateral damage to civilians from drive-by shootings and bombings had claimed thousands of innocent lives.

No way in hell was Stone going to let that happen here.

He drove for fifteen minutes or so, the road snaking alongside various trout streams that flowed quick enough to never ice over in the winter, until he saw the neon sign for Blaine's.

The billiard hall was an anomaly, a lone business on a desolate stretch of road. The place had started life as a convenience store, then been transformed into a honky-tonk strip club that went under before the girls even got their first paychecks, and then finally got converted into a pool hall with an OTB outlet. Local rumors insisted that it was run by organized crime, but Stone doubted even the most desperate mob underling would bother with this dung heap.

Stone pulled into the lot that was more potholes than pavement and parked his Blazer near a row of Harleys lined up by the entrance. Some of the bikes were clean like they hadn't been ridden in a week, but others were spackled with mud and salt from the road. Riding in the winter was dirty business. Not to mention damn cold.

As he stepped into the bar, Stone smelled the universal watering hole stench of spilled beer, cigarette smoke, and Lysol hanging in the air. He could make out the shapes of a dozen men: four hanging around a pool table, three at the bar, and the rest scattered among the tables arranged haphazardly around a dance floor. Since dance floors and billiards didn't really jibe, Stone figured it was a leftover relic from the joint's honky-tonk days.

At Stone's entrance, a biker rose from the nearest table. Big boy, three hundred pounds if he weighed an ounce. He blocked Stone's path.

"Sorry, partner," he said, his gruff voice not sounding sorry at all. "Private club. You need to leave."

"Think I'll stick around," Stone said, flashing his badge. "I need to talk to whoever's in charge."

"Blaine's not here right now. Leave a card and I'll have him call you later."

"I don't mean in charge of this place, I mean in charge of the Children."

The man snorted. "What business you got with the Children?"

"I'll take that up with the head honcho and I'm willing to bet that's not you."

The man scowled as if he'd been insulted, but Stone remained confident this big lummox was nothing more than an enforcer. He exuded bodyguard hostility, not top dog vibes. Still, a pack watched their own, and his posturing had alerted some of the bikers who now drifted closer.

Stone wasn't afraid of a fight, but twelve against one weren't great odds, even for someone skilled in hand-to-hand combat. Maybe he should have brought backup, but it was too late for that now. If things got ugly, he could always use his Glock as an equalizer, but that would be a last resort. He had come here for a chat, not a gunfight.

A man stepped forward. "I'm the club president." He was a little smaller than the rest, broad-shouldered with a shaved head and goatee. The others stepped aside, clearing a space for him. Like everyone else, he wore a sleeveless black leather vest emblazoned with the club's colors.

"I'm Lucas Stone, county sheriff."

"You can call me Roy." The biker didn't offer a last name. He glanced at the men standing around. "Back down, boys. No need to be inhospitable. Sheriff, care for a beer?"

"I'll take a Jack and Coke, lots of ice, easy on the Jack."

Roy smirked. "Not exactly the most manly of drinks."

"Wasn't aware I needed to prove something."

"You don't," Roy said. "But I have to admit, I'm a little surprised that you're drinking on duty. Thought that was against the rules."

"I don't always follow the rules."

"Now that's what I like to hear." Roy turned to the big brute who had blocked Stone at the front door. "Tiny, fetch me a Bud and get our sheriff a Jack and Coke made for a girl." He turned back to Stone. "Let's find a seat and talk like civilized men."

"Thanks." Stone caught some of the bikers looking

bemusedly at his rattlesnake-banded Stetson as he followed Roy to a booth. The Adirondacks weren't exactly cowboy country.

They sat silently, each eyeballing the other, until their drinks arrived.

Roy broke the silence. "So, sheriff, what can the Children do for you?" He leaned hard on the club name as if to remind Stone where he was and who he was dealing with, then took a sip of beer.

"One of your members was killed yesterday," Stone said. "Rammed by a trucker."

"Roger Dorey. A real asshole. Works for Cardine Trucking up the road in Milford. Last I heard, you had him in lockup over in Whisper Falls."

"That's right."

"Maybe you should let him out," Roy said, his razor-thin smile adding a silent implication: *If you do, he'll never make it to court.*

Stone said, "I wanted to ask you about your guy."

"Bobby."

"Did he know anyone at Cardine Trucking?"

"We *all* know people at Cardine. And at Milford Transport. We're a brotherhood of the road," Roy explained. "Bikers, truckers, short-haulers, long-haulers, bus drivers…it's all life on the open road. When it comes to the pavement pounders, everybody pretty much knows everybody around here."

A cagey answer, elegantly vague. Roy might be a badass biker, but he also had some brains bouncing around in his skull. Stone decided to push him a little.

"Mind telling me why your boys are shadowing me?"

"No idea." Roy shrugged. "But if any of my posse are misbehaving, just say the word and I'll stomp it out like a dropped cigarette. We're not interested in trouble with the cops."

"You're telling me you didn't send somebody after me yesterday?"

"I'm telling you my guys—" he gestured around the room at the bikers, "have a will of their own and they tend to get really pissed off when a brother gets run down. If they had their way, we'd all ride into Milford and burn Cardine to the ground."

"That would be a mistake."

"So would killing any more of our members."

Stone leaned forward. "Give it to me straight, Roy."

"I *am* being straight with you."

"Is there bad blood between Cardine and the Children? Anything that might explain why one of their truckers would run down one of your guys?"

Roy shrugged again. "I don't know what was going on between Bobby and Dorey," he said, and it at least sounded honest. "Could have been anything."

"Was he dealing?"

Roy's face darkened. "We don't touch drugs. Not our thing and I don't permit it in my club. If the boys want to smoke a little green stuff on their own time, that's their business. But dealing – even weed – will get you kicked out. We don't want drug dealers riding with the Children." He shot Stone a twisted grin. "Ruins the family-friendly image we're trying to cultivate."

Stone glanced around at the stripper poles, liquor bottles, and rough-looking hell-raisers watching him with baleful eyes. "Yeah, this is a perfect place to take the kids."

"Judge us if you want, sheriff, but we call this place home."

"I'm not judging," Stone said. "I leave that to God." He drained his drink and stood up. "Thanks for your time."

"Just remember I cooperated with you. That's all I

ask." Roy tapped a finger against his beer bottle. "I'll have a word with the boys about Cardine and make sure you don't pick up any more tails."

"Appreciate it."

Stone headed for the parking lot. No one got in his way or said a word. He made it to his Blazer without incident. He was just starting to think this whole visit had gone better than expected when something made him glance back at the billiards hall.

Roy stood just outside the entrance, an amused smile on his face. The smile grew shark-mouth-wide when another man stepped up beside him.

It was the biker Stone had tangled with last night.

Roy gave him a mocking wave that Stone did not return.

Back in town, Stone found himself craving a few minutes of peace and quiet, so he headed for the church instead of the station. He often dropped in here when he felt the need to disappear. With his truck parked around back and out of sight, nobody knew he was here, and he could grab some solitude.

He brewed a cup of coffee in the kitchenette, carried it to his office, and settled down at his desk. Glancing out the window, he could see gray clouds creeping over the high peaks and starting to suffocate the sky. They let him know, along with the chill in the air, that winter wasn't done with the North Country just yet. He was no meteorologist, but he was willing to bet there would be fresh snow on the ground later tonight.

He turned his mental attention to the investigation. He needed to take another crack at Dorey, he needed to talk to Hauser if the man ever came out of his coma, and he needed more background on the relationship between the Children and the Cardine Trucking Company.

There was also the matter of Yankee Doodle Dandy's body. Stone had assigned Drummond, one of his senior deputies, to take point on the Andrew Irwin case. But the man was hardly a crack investigator and sooner or later Stone would have to get involved. So in addition to trekking out to Milford to talk to the people at Cardine, he needed to contact Irwin's commanding officer and see if any of the military backstory connected the kid's death to the broader picture.

No rest for the wicked, Stone thought. Not that he really believed he was wicked. More like a good man who sometimes did wicked things for the right reasons.

He heard the front door of the church open and someone called out, "Stone? You here?"

He recognized the voice of David White, the church's head deacon, and gritted his teeth. White had been a pain in the ass ever since Stone rode into town. Having failed to prevent Stone from getting hired, he now contented himself with taking petty pot-shots at the preacher. It didn't help that the deacon had romantic designs on Holly and was jealous of Stone's relationship with her.

Stone kicked himself for coming to the church. Not that he could have known he would run into White, but talking to the sanctimonious son of a bitch was about as attractive as a root canal without anesthesia. That said, grumbling never solved anything, so best to just get this over with.

"In here, White."

The deacon, a stern-faced man in his mid-fifties and crowned with a mane of black, gray-flecked hair, let himself into the office and took a seat uninvited. "Glad I caught you. I've been meaning to talk to you about the Pressfield presentation the other night."

"Interesting, right?"

"Not the adjective I would use." White raised his chin. "Stone, I wish you had run the idea of hosting him by the deacon board. You must be aware of Pressfield's reputation?"

"He's an expert on extremism. That's why I invited him."

"No, I mean his other reputation. As a champion of far-right ideology."

"His presentation was about the *dangers* of the radical right."

"It's a wolf-in-sheep's-clothing strategy. Make us think he's one thing when he's really another."

"If that's the case, what's his end goal?"

"To distract us from his real agenda."

"And what's that?"

White sighed in exasperation. "Pressfield is part of the radical right! Why can't you see that?"

Stone finished his coffee and stood up. "So let me get this straight. You're saying Homer Pressfield is secretly part of the radical right."

White nodded.

Stone shrugged on his wool-lined rancher's coat. "And he camouflages his beliefs by warning people about the dangers...of the radical right."

White squirmed in his chair as if fire ants had crawled into his boxers. "Well, it sounds stupid when you say it like that."

Stone picked up his Stetson and settled it on his head before heading for the door. Over his shoulder he replied, "You said it, White. Not me."

TEN

STONE'S CELL phone rang as he swung the Blazer into his parking spot at the sheriff's station. He killed the engine and answered the call.

"Hey, Luke. Just checking on you." Holly sounded a little out of breath, like she'd just finished bussing a bunch of tables. Stone could hear the sounds of the diner in the background. "How're things going?"

"Depends who you ask," Stone said, glad to hear her voice. Not for the first time, he admitted to himself that sooner or later, he was going to have to figure out if he wanted to deepen their friendship into something more. But as the saying went, today was not that day and tomorrow wasn't looking good either.

"By the way," he said. "I forgot to tell you earlier, but Yankee Doodle Dandy hitched his last ride. We found his body out near the diner last night."

"I heard about that. Poor guy."

"Be careful out there. We don't know who killed him yet, so keep your eyes open and your gun close. Better safe than sorry."

"That's my motto." Despite the grim news, she still sounded cheerful. "Hey, got dinner plans?"

"Hadn't thought about it."

"Come over to the house. We'll order pizza and watch a movie."

Yeah, someday I have to figure this Holly thing out.

"Sounds good." They said their goodbyes and he dropped the phone back into his coat pocket.

As he crossed the parking lot to the front door, a few fat, lazy snowflakes fell from the iron-colored sky. Looked like they were going to get some white stuff sooner than expected. It happened with wearying regularity. Whisper Falls was situated in the middle of a snow-belt in which storms swept off Lake Ontario and blitzed eastward toward the coast, catching the town right in their path. Sometimes Whisper Falls would get hit with a quick six inches of fresh powder while Saranac Lake, just ten miles away, didn't get so much as a dusting.

Deputy Valentine looked up from his desk as Stone entered. He looked like he wanted to say something, but before he could spit it out, Stone started talking.

"I want our guys alert to any movement by the Children. I want all sightings reported with dates, times, locations, and nature of activity. We need to figure out what they're up to. I'll have Drummond set up surveillance on their clubhouse."

Valentine said, "Speaking of Drummond..."

"What about him?"

"He's in your office with our visitors."

"What visitors?"

"The feds are here."

"Who the hell called them?" Stone frowned and headed for his office.

He walked in to find Deputy Drummond fuming by the window, clearly pissed off. A large man in a trench coat stood nearby, leaning against the wall with an impassive expression on his lantern-jawed face. A woman occupied the chair behind Stone's desk, looking to all the world like she owned the place.

Stone stayed in the doorway, glancing at all the players in the room before finally settling his gaze on Drummond. "Deputy, you want to tell me what's going on?"

Drummond, a short, balding man with a gray moustache, ground his teeth. "Sheriff, I was working on the Irwin murder when these two jerk-weeds came in and seized my notes."

Stone came forward, placed both hands on the desk, and leaned toward the woman. "Who are you and why are you in my chair?"

"I was waiting for you, sheriff." The woman stood up, her movement slender and sinuous, arranging her limbs with the flexibility of a yoga instructor or martial artist. Blonde hair fell past her shoulders and her wide eyes reflected a light that was cold and cast-iron gray. She flashed a badge. "Supervisory Special Agent Tanya Bester, FBI. I'm taking over your investigation."

"Which one?" Stone edged past her and reclaimed his chair. "I've got a vandalism case I could use some help on. Somebody spray-painted the Whisper Falls sign at the edge of town so that it now says 'Whisper Balls.' No suspects at this time. Care to take a look at the file?"

She ignored his sarcasm. "What were you doing out at Blaine's Billiards?"

"Why are you questioning me, Agent Bester? Am I a suspect?"

"It's *Supervisory Special* Agent, actually. But we'll let that slide for now." She glanced at her partner. "Benny, why don't you and 'Bulldog' Drummond there wait outside?" She smiled and what would have been an attractive expression on any other woman with her looks came off as cold and a little bit cruel. "The sheriff and I need to have a little pow-wow."

Stone struggled to keep his cool as Drummond stomped out of the room, followed by Bester's sidekick Benny. He noted how smoothly Bester moved in to shut the door behind them, how she turned and leaned back against it with her arms crossed, how instinctively she sought to manage the room. Clearly she was a power player, someone who savored control, and was probably accustomed to having it most of the time.

To show that he wasn't impressed, Stone swung his booted feet up on the desk. He stared at the agent, waiting for her to make the next move.

Bester walked toward him and reached into her inside jacket pocket, exposing the butt of the automatic holstered in a shoulder rig. Stone couldn't decipher make and model, but it wasn't a small gun. Bester packed big heat.

"Last night your deputies tripped over a body." She withdrew two folded pieces of paper. "Andrew Irwin, age twenty-one."

"Not 'tripped over.' *Found*."

"Whatever." Bester's facial expression indicated her annoyance. "Cause of death?"

"You seized the investigation." Stone picked up a file and tossed it on the desk in front of her. "Read the report. Blunt force trauma."

"Not your first vehicular homicide this week, was it? And yet you put Bulldog Drummond on it."

"Drummond's a good man," Stone said. "Been a cop longer than either of us."

"He's a dinosaur."

"Guess you never learned respect for your elders."

She ignored the jab, unfolded the papers she had

taken out of her pocket, and pushed them across the desk to Stone. "Found this morning over in Essex County, just past the railroad tracks between Saranac Lake and Ray Brook. Look familiar?"

Stone looked at the two photographs of a body, taken from different angles, lying inert on some marshy ground beside a road.

"Notice anything?" Bester asked.

Stone pushed the pictures back across the desk. "Yeah. Red jacket, white cap, blue jeans."

"Not just a red jacket. A North Face down jacket, same make as the one worn by Irwin. By the way, in case you didn't get around to checking, Irwin was regular Army. He went AWOL last month."

"Let me guess," Stone said. "Your guy is Army too and he's also AWOL."

"On leave, actually. But close enough. Given the similarities between our two victims, our profilers are starting to think we're dealing with a serial killer." Bester paused. "That's why I'm here."

Stone shook his head. "You're dealing with a lot more than that."

ELEVEN

"SO IT LOOKS like we'll be coordinating with the FBI going forward." Stone took a drink from his Jack and Coke, then gave Holly a crooked smile. "Guess we made the big time."

"Seems weird, an FBI agent in our little town." Holly toyed with her wineglass. After pizza, they had decided to forego the movie and have drinks instead. "What's he like?"

"She, actually."

"Cool. So she's just like Jodie Foster in *Silence of the Lambs*."

Stone smiled at the comparison and took another drink. The Jack Lumber Bar was so empty tonight that he felt like their voices were echoing off the walls.

Sandwiched between a furniture shop and a liquor store, the Jack Lumber was a working man's bar. Any white-collar types who showed up were just looking for a walk on the wild side without having to actually risk their lives by going to the Nailed Coffin, a disreputable cutthroat dive located in the rougher part of town. Not that very many white collars frequented Whisper Falls, but sometimes the rich tourists wandered over from the luxury accommodations of Lake Placid to see how the peasants lived.

The bar was basically a long, narrow room with booths down one side, the bar down the other, and a dance floor at the far end next to a jukebox currently cranking out an '80s rock song about living on a prayer. The décor was lumberjack chic, with rusty saws and old photos of loggers adorning the walls.

The only other customer was Slidell, sitting in a booth near the juke and slurping on a martini while he muttered into a cell phone.

"Not sure 'cool' is the word I would use," Stone said. "I think I'd prefer Agent Starling to the one I got."

"You mean your new agent-lady-friend isn't some winsome yet determined underdog?"

"She's gives off more of a Gestapo vibe, actually."

"Sounds like you're intimidated by women with power." The mischievous glint in Holly's eye let Stone know she was just teasing.

"Hardly. I hang around with you."

"I'm a waitress, Luke. Not exactly a position of power."

"To someone craving the best bacon cheeseburger in town, you're a queen."

As they chuckled, the bartender wandered over to check on them. He was a tall, thin Black man with a shaved head and diagonal scars swiped across part of his face from a long-ago encounter with a grizzly bear. Skip 'Grizzle' Travers was a fixture in Whisper Falls who kept the peace in the Jack Lumber with the help of his sage-like wisdom and a shotgun loaded with rock-salt that he kept within easy reach beneath the bar.

"This man bothering you, Holly?" Grizzle joked. "Just

say the word and I'll throw him out on his holier-than-thou backside."

"Shame on you, Griz," Holly said with a smile. "Luke is a representative of our legal system."

"That don't mean squat. Not all representatives of the legal system are decent." Grizzle ran a rag over the bar as he shot a sour look at Slidell. Grizzle was not one to engage in gossip – despite knowing half the secrets in town – or insults, but Stone had heard him refer to the lawyer as 'that snake Slidell' more than once. "But if their money is the right color, well..." The barkeeper shrugged. "Who am I to turn away paying customers?"

Before Stone could respond, he felt the air start to vibrate. Moments later, a throaty thunder rumbled down Main Street.

"Harleys," he said. "Headed this way."

"Great." Grizzle shook his head, opened a drawer by the cash register, and took out a short leather cosh. Stone knew the leather-sheathed cudgel was stuffed with ball bearings. As a knockout weapon went, it got the job done. Grizzle set it on a shelf below the bar.

The mechanical roar of the motorcycles rose and crested on the street outside before cutting out. Stone glanced at Slidell. The lawyer had put away his phone and watched the door with interest.

Moments later, a half dozen Children walked into the bar.

Stone recognized the one in front. And from the look on the biker's face, he recognized Stone, too.

"Friend of yours?" Grizzle asked.

"We met yesterday." Stone flexed his aching right hand.

The biker turned and muttered something to his buddies. They were a hairy, ragged bunch, that was for sure. Stone shifted so he was balanced on the edge of his seat with one foot on the floor, braced for trouble.

With zero situational awareness, Slidell chose that moment to ooze into the space between Stone and Holly. "Ah, sheriff, what an unexpected surprise, meeting you here." He gestured for a refill.

The bikers scowled and took up residence at the far end of the bar.

"And Holly!" Slidell gushed. "How are you? It's been so long…"

Holly grimaced. "Hello, Scott," she greeted curtly.

"How have you been?" Slidell lounged on the bar, facing Holly, deliberately putting his back to Stone.

Stone and Grizzle shared a look. The bartender rolled his eyes.

"Fine, thanks." She smiled, big and fake. "Still chasing ambulances?"

Slidell chuckled and seemed to brush off the cheap shot. "That's a rather unkind characterization of my profession. But I understand. A visit with a lawyer is about as welcome as a root canal."

"A date with a lawyer is even worse," Holly said, raising her glass to take a sip of wine.

"Please, Holly." Slidell smirked over his shoulder at Stone. "We wouldn't want to make the sheriff jealous now, would we?"

"We're just friends," Stone said, while something inside called him a liar. "Holly can date whoever she likes." He paused. "Which means you're shit out of luck."

Holly hid her smile behind another drink of wine. Slidell shrugged, dropped some money on the bar, and crawled away with his fresh martini.

Stone looked at Holly. "Did you actually date him?"

"We went on one dinner date, not long after Lizzy and I got here. We weren't even halfway through our salads before I knew I had made a terrible mistake." She shook her head. "He was definitely a one-and-done."

Stone grinned. "You have terrible taste in men."

"Looks who's talking, buddy."

"Want to get out of here?"

"Sounds good."

As they rose to leave, the biker Stone had tangled with perked up, nudged his two nearest pals, and sauntered over.

"Not so fast," he growled, fixing his hostile eyes on Stone. "I got business to settle with you."

"What business is that?" Stone dropped his hands into the pockets of his coat, his right fist curling around the butt of the Colt Cobra.

"You owe me six hundred dollars."

"For what?"

"You busted the mirrors on my hog, that's what. Those were a custom job – design, welding, mounting. You broke 'em, you pay for 'em."

"You messed with a cop." Stone narrowed his eyes. "Play stupid games, win stupid prizes."

Stone felt Holly tense up behind him. On the other side of the bar, Grizzle flicked his eyes from the biker to Stone and back again before discreetly grasping the shotgun.

The biker stepped nose-to-nose with Stone. "You just call me stupid, boy?"

This showdown was clearly going to escalate, so Stone went ahead and escalated it on his terms. He drove his knee into the biker's balls. He got them good too, smashing them up against the pelvis bone. The biker's eyes bugged out and his face turned ghastly white. He collapsed like a pile of bricks, clutching his brutalized manhood.

His nearest pal barreled in, throwing haymakers.

They were street-brawl punches, totally lacking in tactical finesse. Stone easily dodged or blocked them as he backed off, one hand behind him to steer Holly out of the way.

By now the rest of the crew had taken note of the fracas and were beginning to migrate toward them.

"C'mon!" howled the puncher. "Let's see you try 'n kick my nuts! C'mon!"

Stone faked left, ducked right, then drove in with a clean, straight, karate-perfect punch. The first two knuckles impacted with all his weight behind them, propelled by his pivoting hips. He powered through as if trying to slam his fist right out the back of the guy's skull. The hard-driving blow smashed the man in the mouth, hammered his front teeth right out of the gums, and knocked him backward off his feet. He fell into a clutch of barstools, scattering them as he sank into his own personal oblivion.

Stone gritted his teeth against the pain. The punch had hurt his already-injured hand. When this was over, he was going to need more Jack than usual and copious amounts of ibuprofen.

But first he had to end this fight.

The next guy surged forward. The rest of the gang was right behind him and closing fast. Not wanting to use his throbbing fist again, Stone drew his Colt and slashed it across the man's lower jaw right where it hinged. Gunmetal cracked against splintering bone and the biker went down in a pistol-whipped mess. He would be eating through a straw for the foreseeable future.

Grizzle fired his shotgun into the ceiling.

The herd of bikers came to a screeching halt.

Grizzle lowered the muzzle so that it was aimed at the angry mob. "I will shred the next man that moves," he growled in a tone that practically begged any of them to muster up the courage to try.

Stone had the Colt leveled, hammer cocked back. "Who wants to die first?"

The nearest biker held up his hands, shook his head, and stepped back. "Y'all ain't worth taking a bullet for, man." The rest followed suit.

Stone lowered the hammer but kept the revolver out and ready. "Let's go," he said to Holly, and they made their way to the door.

As they exited out into the cold night, Stone's last sight was of Slidell circulating among the bikers, offering condolences and business cards all around.

TWELVE

"THEY WERE IDIOTS, Max, but there were a lot of them. But thanks to Sam Colt and Griz's shotgun, I was able to get out of there without getting stomped."

Max gave him a look that seemed to say, *You should have pissed on them after you knocked them down.*

They were sitting out on the front porch while Stone savored his morning coffee, steam rising from the mug. The snow had stopped overnight, leaving behind a couple inches of fresh powder, and the day had dawned bright and sunny. So bright, in fact, that Stone was thinking about fetching his sunglasses.

But before he could do that, Max stiffened beside him.

A moment later the Shottie sprang to his feet. Stone put a calming hand on the dog's hackles. They both heard the sound of a vehicle coming up the driveway, fresh snow and frozen gravel crunching under the tires.

"Damn early for visitors," he muttered.

A white Range Rover emerged from the tall pine trees that lined the lower half of his driveway and rumbled up toward the house. Stone recognized Agent Bester, wearing the kind of aviator shades that would have made

Tom Cruise proud back in his *Top Gun* days, behind the wheel.

She parked in front of the garage, exited the vehicle, slammed the door with way more force than necessary, and strode toward Stone and Max with her trademark tough-girl smirk cemented in place.

This little lady is dangerous, Stone thought. She moved like a trained fighter, a Muay Thai kickboxer maybe. Stone could tell her hard edge was no feminist façade. This woman sought out conflict, relished measuring herself against opponents to sharpen her skills and resilience. Stone doubted she had ever backed down from a fight in her life.

"Morning, sheriff. Ready for a ride out to Milford?"

"Sure. Coffee?"

"Never touch the stuff. It's slow poison."

"I've been drinking it for thirty years and I'm not dead yet."

"Give it time." Bester shot him a look over the top of her shades. "You probably smoke too."

"Negative. Just a little Jack and Coke now and then."

"How very 'cowboy' of you. I'm guessing you listen to country music."

"That a crime?"

"In certain parts of New York, it is." She smiled, lightening up a bit as she examined the surrounding woodland, hands on her hips. "Nice place you got here. Even got the dog, I see. No woman?"

"Divorced. You?"

"Not divorced." She left the ambiguity hanging in the air and Stone didn't push. Partly because it was none of his business and partly because he just didn't care. Maybe she was a lesbian, or maybe she was one of those women who denied themselves any sexual pleasure, sublimating that energy to other pursuits.

Like becoming a Supervisory Special Agent. Stone knew that took some doing. You had to bring down some top-tier bad boys to get that chair.

"So what's your specialty, Agent Bester? Homicide?"

"Serial murder. Criminal profiling."

"Been at it long?"

"It was my team that caught Butcher Block O'Brian."

"The sick bastard that skinned and fileted his victims while they were alive, right in his kitchen?"

"Yep. Real nasty piece of work." She cocked her head and brought back the smirk. "Sure you're not intimidated working with one of the top detectives in the country?"

"You sure you're not intimidated being out here in the wilds of the Adirondacks? No four-lane highways, no organic grocery stores, not a Starbucks to be had for miles…"

She arched an eyebrow. "You saying this lady can't hang here in cowboy country?"

Stone recognized the goad for what it was – a demand to be taken seriously as a peer. He respected that and he respected her. She was a professional and a specialist, someone with an investigative lens that would complement his own. He expected they would work well together.

Stone rose from his chair, chucked the rest of his coffee into the snow, and smirked back at her. "If you think you can hang, prove it."

———

They took Bester's Land Rover. The drive along State Route 3 to Milford was just over thirty miles, the road gently twisting and turning its way through the mountains, rocky outcroppings rising up every so often. The rocks themselves, beneath sheaths of ice, were gunmetal gray. High up in the cerulean sky, a lone hawk circled.

"So we've got two Army guys, dressed identically, both hitchhiking, both killed on the same stretch of highway," Bester said as she navigated the road like she'd been born in the North Country. "And at least one had a conflict with the local biker gang."

"Maybe that conflict somehow carried over to the other hitchhiker," Stone said. "But why were they dressed the same? Some kind of covert military uniform?"

"I doubt it." Bester shook her head. "The Bureau has a liaison with domestic military law enforcement. They ran the names of both men. Neither one of them has any connection to covert missions or military intelligence."

Stone knew from personal experience that there were plenty of covert missions that got greenlit outside the system, the kind of missions that wouldn't show up on a routine database search by regular military law enforcement. But he didn't bring it up, because his warrior past was not something he intended to discuss with Agent Bester.

The landscape flattened a bit, the road straightening, with fewer curves and more open ground. The Range Rover crested and dipped over rolling hills as the road cut through a cluster of small farms.

Stone saw a long, fallow field patrolled by skulking crows. A single oak stood in the center, barren branches clutching toward the winter sun as if starved for warmth. Between the icy field, black birds, and twisted tree, the whole place had an air of desolation. But Stone knew that would all change once spring arrived and with it, the promise of new life.

"Maybe the outfits are some kind of signal," he said. "An affiliation of some kind."

"Or maybe a signal to get picked up." Bester replied as Milford's skyline materialized on the horizon. "You said your witness, the waitress – what's her name?"

"Holly. And her daughter, Lizzy."

"Yeah, them. You said they saw one or possibly both of our victims hitchhiking regularly past the diner. So maybe these guys were counting on planned transport, like a trucker assigned to pick them up and told to identify them by their clothing."

"Why?"

"Keeping to some kind of schedule is my guess."

He mulled it over as the countryside gave way to the outskirts of Garrison County's urban grease-pit.

The town of Milford was a depressing place Stone avoided as much as possible. Situated right at the northeastern edge of his jurisdiction, just before Garrison County turned into Clinton County and about ten miles outside of Plattsburgh, the place was an ugly smear of industrial warehouses and dying strip malls surrounding a choked downtown of worn shops and low-rent housing. Nearly 7,000 unfortunate souls called Milford home but most of them commuted to Plattsburgh or hopped the ferry across Lake Champlain over to Burlington to find work.

It was also the county seat, complete with a small brick courthouse that looked like it had been built right around the time of the American Revolutionary War. The town's homeless problem took care of itself in the winter months – too cold for sleeping on the cracked and buckled sidewalks – but the vagrants returned in the warmer months like birds migrating north.

Stone much preferred the mountains, woodlands, and high mesas that made up the vast majority of Garrison County. As far as he was concerned, Milford was a concrete eyesore.

Cardine Trucking's headquarters lurked a half a mile off the I-87 North access ramp, on the outskirts of town. Bester parked across the road on a wide industrial access boulevard. The trucking company was located in a long, low-slung building fronted by a series of rolling metal shutters – a cheap alternative to electronic garage doors.

As they got ready to exit the Range Rover, Stone noticed Bester adjusting the fit of her shoulder holster and asked, "What're you packing?"

She smoothly drew the sidearm, making sure the long barrel was tilted toward the floor. The thing was a fucking hand cannon.

"Not standard issue," Bester said, stating the obvious. "But my carry of choice. She's a .44 Auto Mag. Stainless steel chassis with wood furniture grips, a single-stack, seven-round magazine chambered with .44 Xtreme armor-piercing ammo."

"That's a whole lot of gun," Stone remarked.

"Damn straight." Bester slid the huge weapon back into its holster. Even tucked high and tight under her arm, the barrel still touched her waist. "One round of this at center mass will put down pretty much anything. Hell, I could probably drop a rhinoceros with this bad girl."

"Not too many rhinos around here."

Bester opened her door and stepped out. "Pays to be prepared for anything."

Stone circled around the Range Rover and joined her, letting out a little chuckle.

"What's so funny?" she asked.

"I was just thinking about how female FBI agents are portrayed in the movies. You're always wearing high heels."

Bester glanced down at her footwear – a pair of black, retro-styled sneakers. "Kind of hard to chase down and

tackle some asshole against the hood of a car in heels,"
she said.

"I'll bet."

They crossed the street and approached the glass
office door below the hand-painted sign that read 'Cardine Trucking and Transport, Ltd., Est. 2002.' Bester
pushed through into an office reception area that was
conspicuously empty. Stone noted the thin coating of
dust on the hooded computer terminal. A cobweb formed
a triangle in the upper portion of a narrow doorway. A
wider doorway led into a trucking bay.

"Hello?" Bester called out. Receiving no answer, she
made for the trucking bay door, Stone two steps behind.
A clutch of men in mechanic overalls were huddled
together having a chat, but they paused when Bester and
Stone walked in.

"Hello, boys," she said, the rubber soles of her
sneakers squeaking slightly on the grease-stained
concrete floor as she stepped forward and flashed her
badge. "FBI here to pay you a little visit. Keep your
hands where I can see them and line up over there for
me, single file. Let's go."

Nobody moved.

Bester drew her Auto Mag and fired into the ceiling.
The roar of the hand cannon echoed like the crack of
doom in the confined space. Some of the men winced in
pain as the muzzle-thunder pounded their eardrums.

"Don't let the looks fool you, boys. I'm a real bitch
when I don't get my way and I have zero problem
blowing holes in a couple of you to ensure compliance,"
Bester snapped. "So giddyup and form a line before I get
really pissed off."

In short order, the men were exactly where Bester had
ordered them to be and ranged in a single file. Never

underestimate the persuasiveness of large-bore firepower, Stone thought.

"Much better." Bester holstered the gun, clasped her hands behind her back, and studied the line. "Which one of you is in charge?"

Silence for several moments, then one guy spoke up.

"What're you gonna do if we all just keep our damn mouths shut, lady? You can't kill us all."

"Looks like we have a volunteer." Bester marched up to the speaker. "I need to see the scheduling manifest for the past two weeks and I want the log sheets and receipts for every one of your truckers." She gave him a hard-eyed stare. "I may not kill you, but I'll kill your business. No trucks are leaving this facility until further notice. Got it?"

"Leave him alone." Another man stepped forward, this one a shaggy, bearded, longhaired forty-something who looked harried as hell. He glanced left and right at the men lined up on either side of him. "I'll get you everything you want."

"Thanks." Bester stepped aside and the shaggy guy headed toward the office. "What's your name?" she asked, following him while Stone brought up the rear.

"Rohmer," the man answered. "Skip Rohmer. I'm the general manager."

Stone noted that the line of men had not broken up and dispersed. Instead, they trailed them toward the office. There was nothing overtly threatening in their actions, but it still put Stone on edge. He dropped his hand closer to his holstered Glock.

Rohmer stepped into the office, followed by Bester. Stone lingered in the doorway, positioning himself sideways so he could keep an eye on the group of truckers. They paused a dozen paces off, grouped in a rough half-circle, facing toward him.

Rohmer went over to a filing cabinet that looked old enough to have seen service during World War II and banged up enough to have suffered a direct hit from a kamikaze airplane. He opened a drawer and began rifling through various folders while Bester stood on the other side of the counter and waited for him to produce the requested documents.

Instead, Rohmer turned around with a Colt .45 in his fist, pointed right at Bester's face.

Even as Stone's hand reached for his gun, his mind calculated the odds. He was a quick draw, but not rattlesnake fast. And rattlesnake fast was what it would take to put a bullet in Rohmer before he put one between Bester's eyes. He pulled his hand away from the Glock.

Rohmer snarled, "Both of you need to get the fuck out of my garage."

Stone couldn't see Bester's face, but he saw her shoulders stiffen. Somehow he doubted it was from fear. You didn't become an SSA in the FBI without having faced your share of lethal threats. No, more likely the tension in her frame was because she was seething mad at having a gun pointed at her.

As if to confirm his evaluation of the situation, she spoke to him without turning around, her voice cool and calm while her eyes no doubt fired bolts of fury at Rohmer. "Stone, how many of these mutts can you take out?"

Stone shrugged, following her lead and playing it cool, too. "All of them," he said matter-of-factly.

"That's what I like to hear."

"But not before you eat a bullet."

"Dammit, Stone, that's *not* what I like to hear."

"Walk away, Bester. Live to die another day."

The FBI agent spat a curse with enough venom to shame a cobra pit, then growled at Rohmer, "You win this round, asshole, but you know I'll be back with a hundred men to tear this place apart. You and this fucking company are going down."

"Don't matter now." Rohmer smiled thinly. "It's already done. Now get out before I put a bullet in your brain, bitch."

THIRTEEN

STONE SAT in the front seat of the Range Rover, watching Bester as she paced angrily back and forth along the shoulder of the road, cell phone pressed to her ear.

The encounter at Cardine had slapped them both with an unwelcome burst of adrenaline. Stone burned his off by doing some deep breathing exercises. Bester, on the other hand, had gone DEFCON-1 and called her superiors at the Albany field office and loudly demanded that all sorts of warrant-backed ass-kicking commence immediately.

As Stone watched through the windshield, Bester finally paused and began nodding emphatically. She pointed back down the road toward Milford as if whoever was on the other end of the phone could actually see her, then nodded again and hung up before marching to the Rover.

"Okay," she said as she opened the door and climbed behind the wheel. "My people are on it. They'll coordinate with the State Police to execute a full tactical response on Cardine first thing tomorrow morning. Until then, the Bureau is going to keep eyes on the place. Should have a surveillance team inserted within a few hours."

"Sounds good," Stone said. Part of him wanted to go home, arm himself with enough firepower to take down Godzilla, and head back to the trucking company for some full-auto payback. But he decided to do things legally...for now. He could always change his mind and go rogue later.

As Bester swung the Rover back onto Route 3, Stone thought back to Rohmer's words.

It's already done.

What the hell did that mean? He stared out the window and watched the cold, desolate farmland roll by, but there were no answers out there.

"Stone, I'm sorry." Bester broke into his thoughts, her words tight and clipped. "We should have brought backup, gone in with a full team."

"No way you could have known," Stone said. "By the way, your little Annie Oakley routine was interesting."

"Save it," Bester growled, but with a smile. "Just like a cowboy to kick a girl when she's down."

"Least it's just a kick. You almost got a bullet in the face."

"Yeah, that definitely would have put me in a bad mood."

"How would we have known the difference?"

Bester whipped her head around to give him a death-stare, saw his grin, and resumed looking out the windshield. "Jerk," she muttered, but she grinned too.

After a few more miles, Stone asked, "You mind if we make a quick detour?"

"Related to the case?"

"No."

"Something personal?"

"Yeah."

Bester shrugged. "Sure. Just tell me where to go."

"Take the next right."

They were about ten miles out from Whisper Falls when they turned down the dirt road, banks of snow pressing in on each side. They drove another couple of minutes and a rundown, single-story house with a small corral and stable appeared.

Stone pointed at the driveway. "Turn in here."

"Friends of yours?" Bester asked, following his directions.

"Nobody lives here. Not that we can tell anyway." Stone climbed out of the vehicle and went around to a small, open-door barn out back.

A young horse – a black Appaloosa stallion with gray spots – stepped out of the barn and into the attached corral. Stone walked over and reached out a hand and the horse responded by nudging him with its velvety muzzle. The visible outline of ribs beneath the Appaloosa's dark coat hurt something deep in Stone's cowboy heart.

"He's doing better than he was." For some reason, Stone felt the need to explain things to Bester. "One of my deputies found him abandoned here, covered in filth and damn near starved to death. We got him cleaned up and take turns coming out here to give him some feed and exercise."

"He got a name?"

"No." Stone glanced over at her. "Why don't you give him one?"

Bester approached the corral, leaning on the fence next to Stone, neither skittish nor repulsed by the earthy aromas. She might be a city girl, but she showed no fear of the stallion.

She examined the Appaloosa for a solid minute, then

turned to Stone. "Rocky," she said. "Like the boxer in the movies. He was an underdog, right? Well, so is this horse."

"Rocky." Stone nodded. "That works."

"Planning on selling him?"

"No." Stone rubbed the stallion's nose. "Few more days and he'll be healthy enough to move, at which point I plan on taking him to my place."

"What about the owner?"

"I don't give a shit," Stone growled. "You inflict this much pain and cruelty on an animal, you forfeit your rights as far as I'm concerned."

"Still," Bester pressed. "What if they come back?"

Stone patted the horse's neck. "They better not," he said, and left it at that.

FOURTEEN

STONE QUICKLY FED and exercised Rocky and then they got back on the road. A few miles outside of Whisper Falls, a bank of dark clouds moved in, blotting out the sun and sealing off the sky. The temperature dropped and light rain spackled the windshield. Bester hit the wipers and cranked up the heat.

"What do you know about The Remnant?" Stone asked.

"The Neo-Nazi group?"

"Yeah."

"Why?" She smirked beneath her aviator shades, which she kept wearing despite the fact that the sun had vanished. "You thinking about joining?"

"Very funny. No, I just have a theory."

"What theory?"

"Remember what Rohmer said right after he got the drop on you?"

Bester shifted in her seat. "I don't want to talk about that again until that sneaky bastard is eating dirt with his hands cuffed behind his back."

"You just want to arrest him? Not kill him?" Stone grinned. "You're getting soft, Agent Bester."

"I don't need him dead. Letting him become some-body's prison bitch is payback enough for me."

"Well, that's nice and all, but do you remember what he said?"

"Yeah," she replied. "He said 'It's already done.' So what?"

"What do you think he meant by that?"

"Not sure, but I doubt it has anything to do with The Remnant."

"Maybe not. Just humor me and tell me what you know about them."

"Fine." Bester paused for a moment as if gathering her thoughts, then started speaking. "Timothy McVeigh started something. When he drove up in front of that Federal Building in Oklahoma, you had a scattered handful of serious players at the white nationalist table. There was Richard Butler and his bunch at Hayden Lake. And, of course, The Order got its fair share of publicity. But the rest? Pretty much just costume clowns and weekend warrior wannabes. Nothing serious."

Stone shook his head. "Oklahoma City was a damned dark day in this country's history."

"FBI had an office in the Alfred Murrah Federal Build-ing. We lost some good agents in that bombing."

"Sorry."

"So am I. But you can bet plenty of beers got hoisted at FBI watering holes all over the country the night that son of a bitch rode the rocket in Terra Haute. Man, we hated that bastard. But sometimes it feels like he's still living and breathing, rising from the dead like some kind of skinhead Jesus to give birth to a bold new age of white nationalism. He might be dead, but his beliefs caught fire. I think The Remnant grew out of that."

"Sparks from ashes, that kind of scenario?"

"The growth in white nationalism and domestic white supremacist terrorism has been exponential since 2001. Back then, there were less than five documented attacks by right-wing extremists in the United States. Last year, that number was forty-five."

Bester turned into Stone's driveway, startling some chickadees from the row of pine trees. As they drove up to the house, a snowshoe hare darted in front of the Range Rover as if one of its buddies had dared it to see how close it could get to the front tires without getting flattened.

"You almost had rabbit stew for dinner," Bester chuckled.

"Wouldn't be the first time," Stone said. "They taste like chicken. And no, I'm not joking."

He invited her inside for a cup of coffee and introduced her to Max, who appeared as aloof as always. Then she sat at his breakfast bar and continued talking while Stone grabbed a couple of mugs from the cupboard.

"Back when The Order killed radio talk show host Alan Berg, armed cells of white nationalists were an anomaly. But today, there are over a dozen copycat organizations. Out of all of them, The Remnant is the most dangerous. The Bureau started tracking them right after we learned of their existence, somewhere around 2016 or 2017. Since then, they've been responsible for at least a dozen murders. You already had groups like Blood and Soil and Atomwäffen willing to kill, but The Remnant used different tactics. They're basically an Aryan suicide squad."

Stone started pouring coffee into the mugs. "That level of fanaticism is hard to come by," he said. "How do they do it?"

"A lot of their members are ex-military." Bester

tapped her temple with a fingertip. "The kind of soldier who comes preprogrammed to obey orders without question."

Stone set a cup of coffee on the counter in front of her. She took a sip, trilled out an appreciative murmur that most men would have found erotic, and then resumed speaking.

"Terrorist groups, as a general rule, have some kind of paramilitary leadership. It's one of the reasons the Feds were so slow to classify McVeigh and his ilk as actual terrorists. Whether the infrastructure existed before or only came into existence after the Oklahoma attack is hard to say. But suddenly white nationalism was on the map in a way it had never been before."

"So what makes The Remnant special?"

"Their degree of sophistication. These people have serious expertise on their side. The Remnant actively recruits out of the military community. They've got people with knowledge of logistics, weapons, intelligence...you name it."

"Which brings me to my theory."

Bester nodded. "I think I'm tracking with you. You're thinking our friends in the red, white, and blue are with them. With The Remnant."

"Like I said, it's just a theory."

"It fits. They're both military. One is AWOL and—"

Her voice trailed off as Max popped up from his dog bed, ears pricked up, and padded over to the front door to let them know someone was coming.

A few moments later the door swung open as Holly let herself in. When she saw them both standing there, she smiled and said, "Sorry, am I interrupting something?"

Stone smiled. Holly had a way of making him do that. "No need to be sorry." He set down his coffee cup.

"Holly, meet Supervisory Special Agent Taryn Bester of the FBI."

"Hello." Holly stepped forward, hand outstretched. Bester grasped it with both her hands and gave Stone's favorite lady the kind of warm smile that he hadn't believed she was capable of generating. Apparently, Bester could turn on the charm when she wanted to.

"We just got back from Milford," Bester said to Holly, letting go of her hand after holding it a few seconds too long. "Had ourselves a bit of an adventure."

Holly looked concerned. "Everything all right?"

"We're fine," Stone said. "Someone just objected to our questions, that's all."

Bester finished her coffee and checked her watch. "I need to get back for a teleconference." She flashed a smile at Holly. "It was nice meeting you."

"Same here."

Bester's eyes lingered on Holly. "Maybe next time I'm in town, I can buy you a drink."

Holly blushed a bit, but said, "Sure. That'd be fun."

"It's a date then." Bester smiled again and kept on smiling as Stone walked her out to the Range Rover.

"I'll coordinate with the team," she said, getting back down to business, "and we'll take another shot at Cardine in the morning."

"Sounds good."

"So, uh, Stone. About Holly…"

"What about her?"

"Is she your…?"

"My what?"

"You know."

Stone grinned and shook his head. "We're just friends."

"Good." Bester dropped her shades back into place as

she climbed into the Range Rover. She headed down the driveway without so much as a wave.

Back inside, Holly was sitting at the same spot at the breakfast bar that Bester had just vacated. "Interesting woman, that Agent Bester," she said.

"Looks like she's got a crush on you."

"Jealous?" Holly teased.

"That's between me and God."

"Maybe I should ask Him then."

"A little prayer never hurt anyone."

Holly looked down at her hands. Stone wondered if she was remembering how it felt to have them held by Bester. When she looked back up, her eyes were serious. "I do pray for you sometimes, Luke," she said softly. "For *us*."

Stone knew they were on delicate ground. He kept his voice as soft as hers when he asked, "God give you any answers?"

She smiled. "I'm sitting in your kitchen, aren't I?"

By some silent, unspoken, mutual agreement, they decided to leave it at that.

———

They chatted for a while and then went their separate ways. Holly had somehow allowed herself to get roped into helping Lizzy bake cookies for a school event. Stone needed to run into town for dog food and a few other supplies.

"Watch yourself around Agent Bester," Holly said before she left. "She views you as competition. She'll probably challenge you to a duel to see which of you wins the rights to my affections."

"You're probably right." Stone grinned. "Lucky for me, I'm pretty good with a gun."

As he drove into town shortly before dusk, Stone reflected on the fact that every undercover operative – man or woman – he'd ever known had ended up having an affair. It was almost like an accessory of the undercover lifestyle. Sometimes it was even a requirement of the role, a necessity for the cover story.

He wondered if Bester had a wife somewhere, a submissive little partner who darned her socks and rubbed her shoulders when she shrugged off her oversized holster. Maybe Bester was chasing a taste of the wild life while out on assignment. She sure had taken a liking to Holly.

Jealous?

He could still hear Holly's voice asking him the question. Alone in the truck, he could answer honestly.

Hell yeah.

Then he forgot all about those kinds of thoughts. Because on the edge of town, where Pine Street intersected with Route 3 before snaking over the back way toward Lake Placid, he saw Yankee Doodle Dandy standing there with his thumb out.

FIFTEEN

STONE PULLED off to the side of the road and killed his lights. The rain had started up again a few miles back, fat droplets falling from the bursting-open belly of the cloud bank above. Not too heavy yet but picking up in intensity.

The wipers swished clean the rain-splattered windshield and gave Stone a good look at the guy. Sure enough, it was a Yankee Doodle Dandy wearing a white cap, red jacket, and blue jeans.

Stone debated calling for backup, but for what? The guy was just standing there on the side of the road. Stone opted to just wait and watch and see what happened.

The rain started coming down harder. The Yankee Doodle looked sodden but patient as he stood there with his thumb out. He wore a black backpack, like all the others, but Stone noticed this guy's was full where the others had all been empty.

Something was up.

A minute later, headlights appeared in Stone's side-view mirror, carving through the twilight murk and the rain which now hammered down in heavy sheets rather than singular droplets. A pickup truck – looked like a green Nissan but it was hard to tell through the deluge – passed Stone's parked Blazer and pulled over on the other side of the road.

Yankee Doodle, shoulders hunched against the downpour, spotted the truck and lowered his thumb.

Stone decided he had watched long enough. Time for action. He climbed out of the Blazer and sprinted across the road.

The rain lashed the earth like God was pissed off at the world again and in a drowning mood. The storm hit with a fury. Visibility plummeted to just a few feet. Moments ago, Yankee Doodle had been a distinct figure just a dozen meters away; now he was nothing more than a shadowy blob blurred by the cold, relentless rain as he moved toward the waiting truck.

Half-blinded from the water whipping into his eyes, Stone moved to intercept. Dimly through the downpour, he saw a door open and glimpsed the smudged glow from the instrument panel. The shadow-shape of the hitchhiker started to climb into the cab.

"Sheriff's department!" Stone yelled. He didn't bother hauling out his badge since they wouldn't be able to see it anyway. "Stop right there!"

Like an illusionist pulling off a magic trick, the hitchhiker vanished into the rain. There one second, gone the next. A goddamned ghost.

Stone sensed danger to his left a heartbeat too late. A fist rocketed out of the rain and crashed into the side of his head. He staggered sideways, the buffeting winds knocking him even further off balance.

He reached for his gun. The Colt Cobra .38 snubnosed was right there in the pocket of his soaked rancher's coat. His fingers curled around the grips. As he lifted the revolver out, his boot heel skidded on something wet and slippery.

Already off balance, he went down. His hand bounced against the road and the rain-slick pistol skittered out of his fingers and tumbled across the wet asphalt.

A boot lashed out at Stone. He dodged it. The hitch-hiker darted back into the rain and shadows, using the elements like a cloaking device.

He heard someone snarl a curse. He turned his head and glimpsed movement by the truck. The driver was climbing down.

He also spotted his gun.

The Cobra gleamed on the shoulder of the road. Stone crabbed forward and grabbed for the pistol but received a face full of boot leather for his trouble. The kick thundered against his jaw, and he knew it would leave a nasty bruise. The blow slammed him sideways, the Colt spinning out of reach again.

Stone lashed out blindly with his right boot heel, seeking a target in the storming darkness. He connected solidly with something that felt like a shin or maybe a kneecap. A scream ripped through the air, barely audible over the waterfall-like roar of the rain.

A boot stomped the ground next to his head, missing by a scant inch. He looked up to see the driver raising his boot for another try. Stone rolled to the side. He heard a loud pop followed by a hissing noise.

He rolled one more time and used the momentum to propel him back onto his feet, just as the driver lunged out of the pounding rain again. Stone fired a short, chop-ping punch to the guy's midsection, right below the ster-num. The driver took the blow with a pained grunt and immediately retreated.

Stone managed to find the Colt Cobra. He heard the

sound of an engine revving and realized the driver had made it back to the truck. Through the dark, blinding veil of rain, he saw the red smear of the taillights as the hitchhiker scrambled into the cab and slammed the door shut.

Stone raised his pistol and fired a double-tap but in the downpour, he couldn't see where he hit...if he even hit anything at all. For all he knew, the bullets had zipped across the creek that ran beside the road and buried themselves in the trees on the other side.

The truck raced away and vanished into the storm.

Stone ran back across the road to his Blazer but pulled up when he saw the left front bumper sagging almost all the way down to the pavement. He remembered the pop-hiss he'd heard.

The bastard knifed my tire.

Stone snarled a curse. He didn't even have a plate number, meaning Yankee Doodle and the truck driver had gotten away clean.

The rain started to slacken but it wasn't enough to improve his mood.

———

"That," said New York State Police BCI Detective Jim Spencer, "is one nasty bruise."

Detective Spencer and Agent Bester had responded promptly when Stone called them about the attack. They were now convened at the sheriff's station, finalizing plans for tomorrow morning's raid on Cardine Trucking and Transport while the search was underway for the green truck, the driver, and the hitchhiker.

Stone rubbed his jaw. "Should fade soon enough."

"Heard you were a badass fighter, Stone," Bester said, her tone light and teasing. "But I'm starting to think you're just a *bad* fighter."

Stone shrugged and smiled. "Even the best lose a fight sometimes," he replied. "And I'm not the best."

Spencer's cell phone buzzed. The detective picked it up, swiped the screen, and then turned to Stone. "A trooper found a green truck abandoned out on Route 73 just past the ski jumps. Said there's a bullet hole in the tailgate and another one in the back window." He turned the screen around so Stone could see it. "That the truck?"

Stone nodded. "Yeah, looks like it."

"No sign of the driver or our red-white-and-blue hitchhiker," Spencer said.

Stone swore under his breath. Another dead end.

SIXTEEN

THE LAW ENFORCEMENT presence for the raid on Cardine was so massive that Stone thought it looked like overkill. Clearly Bester had some juice, and she was looking to make a statement.

Two SWAT detachments from local police departments augmented a twenty-man riot squad from the State Police. US Marshals were present – both a plainclothes and combat assault division – to execute a federal warrant since Bester, a federal law enforcement officer, had been threatened with deadly force yesterday.

It was a damn army of ass-kickers, Stone thought as he surveyed the assembled crew, staged up in the sheriff's station garage wearing full tactical gear and armed to the teeth. If Rohmer or anybody else at Cardine Trucking pulled a gun today, they were going to be ventilated with more holes than a Swiss cheese factory.

If that happened, Stone suspected it would be no great loss to the world, even as his preacher side reminded him that all souls were God's children, and their deaths should not be taken lightly. Sometimes the warring duality of his nature bothered him, but mostly he just shrugged it off and kept trying to figure out how to live with it.

As a supervisory agent, Bester was the highest-ranking official on the raid. She waved a hand for silence and once she had it, started giving the men a sit-rep.

"Listen up, gents. I had a gun pulled on me yesterday by the manager of this shithole, a guy named Rohmer. We suspect he and his crew have additional firepower, so we're going in hard."

Somebody in the back cracked a lewd joke. A few guys snickered. Bester ignored them.

"The SWAT teams will cover the north and east sides. Since the rear of the building butts up against a concrete wall, we won't have to worry about that. The State Police will execute a two-pronged assault, breaching through two different doors simultaneously. The marshals will back them up. Any questions on all that?"

Nobody spoke up or raised their hand.

"Speaking of the marshals," Bester said. "They get first dibs on our guys since we are technically executing a warrant from a federal grand jury. But I have been assured we'll get a chance to have a sit-down with Rohmer and his goons before they're hauled off." She turned her head and looked over at Jim Spencer. "Jim, you have anything you want to say?"

"No, we're good to go."

Bester glanced at Stone. "Anything?"

He shook his head. The time for talk was over. Now it was time to hit the road, kick down some doors, and get some answers.

Bester knew it too. "All right, cowboys," she said. "Mount up and let's roll."

The convoy sped down State Route 3 in six vehicles: three black SUVs with tinted windows followed by one State Police car and an unmarked bus with blacked-out windows carrying the riot squad. A black armored personnel carrier emblazoned with the New York State Police seal brought up the rear.

Stone had no doubt that it was the largest law enforcement presence Garrison County had ever seen. He still wasn't convinced it was necessary – an APC to raid a trucking company? – but Bester was calling all the shots on this one and she seemed to subscribe to the bigger-is-better theory.

Stone rode with Spencer and Bester in the lead SUV. They made good time, encountering minimal traffic on the early morning road. No one spoke, each lost in their own thoughts. If anyone had pre-mission jitters, they kept it hidden.

Milford appeared up ahead. It was show time.

They skidded to a stop in front of Cardine Trucking and Transport, their driver twisting the wheel to turn the SUV broadside so they could use it for cover. Stone, Spencer, and Bester exited quickly. Spencer immediately sprinted over to the bus as it rolled to a halt and began directing the riot squad as they spilled out.

"Ready for this, Stone?" Bester wore her aviator shades like some kind of '80s action movie hero and the Auto Mag in her hand just added to the retro look. She seemed almost eager for violence, an adrenaline junkie hungry for a high-profile takedown. Stone generally disliked that type, but Bester wore it well.

"Ready." Stone braced himself against the hood of the SUV. Using a pair of binoculars, he glassed every window and door within his field of vision. No sign of life that he could see.

"All teams, this is Eagle," Bester said into a radio

hand mic. "Stand by." She clicked off and looked at Stone. "Anything?"

"Negative. But that doesn't mean they're not in there, holed up out of sight. Tell our snipers to stay sharp."

"They will." Bester keyed her mic. "Okay, teams, take 'em in."

A moving column of riot police fast-walked toward the side entrance, shields up, covered by black-garbed SWAT operators brandishing Heckler & Koch submachine guns. Another team closed in from the opposite side like a mirror image.

Stone watched as the lead trooper swung a battering ram into the door. The wood around the knob caved in as the door imploded from its hinges. The teams poured in, backed by their SWAT escorts.

Spencer rejoined Stone and Bester behind the SUV and raised his hand-held radio. "Give me a sit-rep ASAP."

The stillness that followed seemed interminable but in reality it was probably no more than ten seconds before the answer came.

"No contact, no resistance. Finishing our sweep but it looks like the place is empty."

Stone headed inside, followed by Bester and Spencer. He found a SWAT guy standing behind the reception desk.

"Nobody?" Stone asked.

"Negative, sheriff. And take a look at this." The SWAT officer used the muzzle of his assault rifle to pry open a drawer. It was empty. "All the drawers are cleaned out. Hell, the whole *place* is cleaned out. They even took the light bulbs."

"Weird," said Bester. "They didn't panic at the last minute and bug out fast. This was a planned evacuation, an orchestrated pullout. Usually you only see this level of evacuation detail with military units and, sometimes, religious cults."

"The Remnant are a bit of both," Stone said.

"Them again." Bester seemed to suddenly realize she was still holding her Auto Mag and quickly jammed it into the holster as she followed Stone out into the empty, cavernous garage space. "You really think they're mixed up in this somehow?"

"Can't rule it out." Stone paused in the middle of a truck bay and watched as teams of officers continued their search of the facility. "We have AWOL soldiers. We know The Remnant recruits from the military. And we have a connection between the truckers, the Children, and the dead hitchhikers."

"Not a connection that will stand up in court, we don't."

"It's a work in progress," Stone replied.

"Excuse me, Agent Bester? Sheriff?" A state trooper waved from across the garage. "Got something you might want to take a look at."

Stone spotted it before they even got there – a stitching of holes along the wall and into the jamb of the garage door.

"Looks like some full-auto action," Bester said.

"Sure does," Stone agreed. "Spray and pray all the way."

Bester frowned. "From the looks of things," she turned and squinted at the center of the garage space, "they fired from somewhere in the middle of the room, angling upward."

"Like at the cab of a truck." Stone walked over to his best guesstimate for where the shooter had stood, followed by Bester. "Someone with an ax to grind showed up as the Cardine crew were vacating the premises and decided to dump some rounds at one of the trucks."

"Shell casings on the floor." Bester crouched down, studying the brass. "Looks like 9mm." She looked up at Stone. "You thinking the Children?"

Stone nodded. "I'm thinking the Children are mixed up with the hitchhikers and The Remnant." He paused, staring at the spent cartridges scattered across the garage floor. "And I think they're at war with the truckers."

SEVENTEEN

STONE RETURNED to his office late that afternoon. As he sat down and thumbed through his calendar, he noted what was scheduled for court tomorrow morning. He slouched back in his chair and let out a half-sigh, half-growl. Going to court was about as much fun as getting a colonoscopy with an ice fishing auger.

The phone rang. He leaned forward and picked it up.

"Sheriff Stone."

"There you are, sheriff. I was beginning to think you were never at your desk."

Stone grimaced. Slidell was about the last person on earth he wanted to talk to right now. "Last time I checked," he said, "most crimes don't get solved sitting behind a desk."

"Ah, yes, I sometimes forget that you fancy yourself a cowboy cop. Stetson on your head, six-shooter on your hip, faithful steed to carry you into the fray, that sort of thing."

Stone growled, "What do you want, Slidell?"

"Just calling to remind you that we have a date in the courtroom tomorrow."

Stone tapped his desk calendar. "Dorey's arraignment. Got it written down right here."

"Are you and the prosecutor prepared to present evidence of this conspiracy you so rashly accuse my client of participating in?"

"You'll found out tomorrow."

"Fine, be that way," Slidell said. "I just wanted to reach out and ensure you'll be present. Of course, you must realize that I will be calling you as one of my prime witnesses."

"It's nice to be wanted. Anything else, Slidell?"

"Say hello to Holly for me, would you?"

Stone could practically see the lawyer's smirk through the phone. He considered driving over to Slidell's office and wiping it off his face with a hammer.

Instead, he just hung up.

———

Stone slept just fine that night. He didn't worry about the arraignment until he walked into the courthouse and saw Slidell talking to Deacon White.

Behind his holier-than-thou piety, White coveted the position of pastor at Faith Bible Church. He also coveted Holly. In other words, he wanted what Stone had and there was little he wouldn't do to bring Stone down. That included allying himself with an unscrupulous snake of an attorney like Slidell. The sight of them huddled up and talking in low, secretive tones about God-knew-what left Stone a bit uneasy.

He was a man of action. He wasn't geared for the verbal warfare of a courtroom battleground. His idea of winning an argument was to put a bullet in the enemy's head before he could return the favor. Stone guessed that tactic wouldn't impress the judge.

He found Mason, the prosecutor, in the hallway. With his shaved head and stocky frame, Mason looked more like a carnival wrestler than a prosecutor. He carried something of that pugnacious attitude into his conduct as Whisper Falls' one-man avenger of injustice.

"What does Slidell think he's doing with David White?" Mason grumbled as he grappled with his briefcases and hauled them into the courtroom. "If being an asshole was a felony, White would be guilty in the first degree."

Stone didn't offer a reply as he took his usual seat alongside Mason at the prosecutor's table. He knew to leave a chair between them for Mason's second and third briefcases.

He had seen plenty of big city district attorneys prosecute crimes with only one briefcase, so he wasn't sure why Mason needed three in little old Garrison County. But nor did he ask, because whatever his methods, the prosecutor got shit done, and that's all that mattered. At least the briefcases all matched.

"What's the play?" Stone asked as Mason piled books and papers on the table in front of him.

"We're going with voluntary manslaughter which I might try to crank up to Murder Three, depending."

"Depending on what?"

"All rise!"

The door to the judge's chambers opened and a small, rotund Hispanic woman wearing a black judicial robe shuffled into the courtroom.

"Court is now in session, the Honorable Bianca Jaramillo presiding."

"Great," Mason muttered under his breath. "It's 'Social Justice' Jaramillo."

Stone knew her by reputation only and that reputation wasn't good. A total hard-ass and a real cop-hater.

"Order in the court. Please be seated."

Judge Jaramillo fiddled with her desk calendar as the clerk announced the case number, then asked, "Who do we have for the defense?" She peered over her glasses. "That you, Scott?"

"It is indeed, your honor."

"So nice to see you again, counselor. Please convey my regards to your sister, if you'll be so kind. I owe her a phone call." The judge shifted in her chair to face the prosecutor's table. "Mr. Mason, tell me what the state contends regarding Mr. Dorey."

"Good morning, your honor." Mason stood up. "Mr. Dorey was witnessed behind the wheel of his work vehicle, in apparent full possession of his faculties, when he suddenly—"

"Objection, your honor," Slidell interjected. "Presupposition by counsel. My colleague has no way of knowing my client's state of mind at the time of the incident."

Stone groaned inwardly. It was going to be a long damn day. Slidell was pulling out all the stops.

"Sustained. The prosecution will confine himself to known facts."

Mason nodded. "Of course. After all, I wouldn't want your honor's conversation with defense counsel's sister to get uncomfortable."

Judge Jaramillo shot Mason a look that could have frozen hellfire. "I'd tread carefully if I were you, counselor."

"Sorry, your honor." He didn't sound sorry at all.

She pinned him with her frosty stare for another few heartbeats, then said, "Continue."

"Thank you, your honor." Mason shuffled some papers. "The defendant, Mr. Dorey, knowingly and willfully accelerated his truck and struck a motorcycle, killing Robert 'Bobby' Anderson, a local biker."

"He was a biker who rode with the Children, wasn't he?" The judge's eyes flashed over top of her glasses again. "Let's not sugar-coat salient facts, such as the deceased's involvement with a notorious criminal gang."

"Of course, your honor. May I continue?"

"Get to the point, Mr. Mason."

"The point is this – the state contends that Mr. Dorey's collision with Mr. Anderson, which resulted in Mr. Anderson's death, was deliberate and intentional, part of a criminal conspiracy to take revenge on the Children by employees of Cardine Trucking and Transport."

"I see. Wow." Judge Jaramillo and Scott Slidell shared a *can-you-believe-this-shit?* look. "That's a bit of a whopper, Mr. Mason. You really should consider a career writing fiction. You're very good at it." She looked at Slidell. "Defense, you want to say your spiel?"

"Yes, thank you, your honor." Slidell rose. "I shall dispense with lengthy preambles and colorful flourishes like my esteemed colleague, Mr. Mason. It is not my purpose to convince your honor of any conspiracies or hidden agendas. But I will put forward that the procedural aspects of this arrest *do* concern us here. I—"

Mason leaned over and whispered to Stone, "Did you read him his rights? Give him food? That sort of thing? Because that's where this is headed."

"The arrest was solid," Stone whispered back.

"You didn't call him a dumb cracker?"

"No."

"Didn't threaten to kill him?"

"No."

"Didn't grab his balls during the pat-down?"

"Wait, that's not allowed?"

Mason smirked.

Slidell, meanwhile, was on a roll.

"There are questions regarding the procedural and policing aspects of this arrest. Your honor, it's highly unusual to question arrest procedures in an arraignment hearing. But I wish to go even further and question the mental competence of the officer involved. That officer being Sheriff Lucas Stone."

"Whoa." Mason shot to his feet. "Hang on a minute. Objection."

"Your honor, the defense is prepared to produce a witness who will attest to recent erratic behavior on the part of Sheriff Stone, related to the sheriff's other duties as pastor of the Faith Bible Church. My witness is prepared to testify that Sheriff—excuse me, *Pastor* Stone —recently invited a speaker to their church with known ties to political extremism."

"That's bullshit," Stone growled. Judge Jaramillo shot him a warning glance but didn't reprimand him for his violation of courtroom decorum.

"Political extremism?" Mason furrowed his brow. "Who are we talking about?"

"Homer Pressfield." Slidell said the name with a triumphant smile.

"Shit." Mason stared at the floor.

"There a problem?" Stone asked.

Mason shrugged. "I'll try to run some damage control but I'm not going to lie, sheriff, this hurts us a little bit." He turned to the judge. "Your honor, I'll need time to confer with the witness. Mr. Slidell never indicated that he intended to put Sheriff Stone on trial for mental competency."

"You've got ten minutes."

"Your honor, that's not enough—"

"Ten minutes!" She smacked her gavel.

"*All rise.*"

Everyone stood as Judge Jaramillo lumbered out of the courtroom.

———

"I need a new head deacon," Stone said. "White's a prick."

"He definitely sucks," Mason agreed.

"Maybe I'll just kill him."

"Delightful as that sounds, as an attorney, I would advise against it."

Mason toasted Stone with his third glass of red wine. Stone responded by raising his second Jack and Coke – this one even easier on the Jack than the first – and the two men drank in the miserable silence of an empty Jack Lumber Bar. The day had not gone well.

"At least you can still work," Mason said. "They didn't shut you down or ask for your badge."

"No, they're just going to audit my department."

"That'll be handled by the Attorney General's office." Mason jerked a thumb at his chest to point at himself. "I've got plenty of pull there and I'll call in some favors. Don't worry, pal, I've got you covered."

EIGHTEEN

STONE WOKE up earlier than usual the next morning, his mind in turmoil, his spirit troubled. He took a quick shower, fed Max, and then headed down to the church for some alone time.

His was an earthy, simple faith. Sure, he had written plenty of essays in seminary about theology, even excelling in topics like grace, incarnation, and the trinity. But they were just papers, of interest only to philosophers and academics. Too many people wanted to study Christ but didn't want to *know* Him.

Stone refused to view Jesus as some abstract perfectionist standing on high, chastising the world while never getting His robes dirty. Despite being pure holiness wrapped in the flesh of a lowly carpenter, Christ roamed among the commoners, spending far more time with the sinners than the so-called saints.

Stone entered the sanctuary and slid into the back row of pews. He fixed his eyes on the large wooden cross hanging behind the pulpit, thinking about everything it represented. Thinking about *who* it represented.

Jesus Christ. The man who died for the sins of the

world. The one who took the nails and paved a way for humanity to find sacred redemption. Because a price had to be paid.

God knew that the key to Heaven for mankind meant putting His son through Hell. There could be no salvation without sacrifice. No paradise without pain. No good without evil.

Good and evil...

Stone knew better than most that there was a whole lot of gray area on the spectrum between righteousness and wickedness. He was a man who believed in justice, and he was a man who believed that justice didn't always operate inside the rigid boundaries of the legal system. Sometimes the law failed.

Thanks to manipulating assholes like Scott Slidell.

It was so hard not to hate the man.

Stone knew that as a man of faith – a preacher, for that matter – he wasn't supposed to hate anyone. The Bible commanded believers to pray for their enemies, not despise them. But sometimes his spirituality rubbed up against his reality. Sometimes faith didn't fix anything; it just caused internal friction.

Stone had done plenty of difficult things in his life. He'd left his family and forged a lonely, duty-bound life as a warrior. He'd once hiked alone across twenty miles of Antarctic ice after a mission went wrong. He'd held the broken, bloodied bodies of his brothers-in-arms and wept unashamedly when his fellow warriors fell in the battle. He had choked on grief as he told fathers and mothers that their son was never coming home.

Yeah, he'd done some hard things.

But praying for Slidell? Yeah, that was a bridge too far.

He gazed up at the cross. *Forgive me, Lord, but I just can't do it.*

There was no thunderous, booming answer. Stone knew God rarely spoke like that. When working with human souls, God typically chose to speak in a still, small voice, a gentle whisper rather than a wrathful roar.

Or, as was the case right now, to not speak at all.

Stone stood up and walked out of the church. If he sat in the pew and waited for God to change his mind, then he'd be sitting there all day, and he didn't have the time for that right now.

He had a horse to save.

———

Sunlight burned off the icy haze that clung to the farmlands between Whisper Falls and Milford. Stone turned down the dirt road, horse trailer bouncing along behind the Blazer, and headed for the abandoned farm where Rocky currently resided.

It was time to give the horse a new home, Stone thought as he turned into the driveway. The Appaloosa stallion deserved a better life than the filth and squalor it had known up until now.

Stone suddenly saw that he was not alone. A long red pickup truck, its chassis shiny and new, was parked by the stables. "What the hell?" he muttered, shifting into park and turning off the ignition.

As he climbed out of the Blazer, Stone heard an angry voice hollering something, followed by a sharp *hiss-crack!* that split the cold morning air. This was followed by a horrible, inhuman cry of agony.

Like any cowboy worth his salt, Stone recognized the sound of a horse in pain.

He ran as fast as he could.

As he skidded around the corner, frozen clods of dirt shifting under his boots, Stone saw that Rocky's pen was open, the Appaloosa secured to a feed trough by a mouth chain. A man stood behind him and off to one side, brandishing a steel-cable stun whip.

Stone saw two red stripes down Rocky's flanks and seriously thought about killing the guy. He didn't draw his Glock because he was afraid the temptation to put a bullet in this bastard's head would be too strong to resist.

"Hey!" he yelled. "Put it down!"

The man turned, fast and quick-footed. Young, early twenties, with close-set eyes and freckles. The whip slashed out at Stone, tearing a strip from the arm of his jacket. The thick padding kept the steel from cutting him open, but it still stung like hell.

Before the whip-man could strike again, Stone bull rushed him.

He drove into the kid full force, ramming with his shoulder. He felt the breath explode out of the guy's lungs in a forced, sudden-impact exhale. Stone slammed him against the barn wall and heard the sharp snapping of ribs.

Stone powered up and punched the guy twice in rapid succession. One shot to the jaw, the other to the temple. They weren't gentle blows. The stun whip dropped to the ground.

Stone finished him off by executing a hard takedown that ended with crunched bones and moans of pain. Moans that became shrill screams when Stone stood up and stomped on the man's right hand, breaking it.

"That'll teach you to whip a horse," he growled. "You ever do it again, I'll break your neck."

"Hey."

Stone turned.

A girl stepped out from the shadows that cloaked the barn's interior. With her Levi's, work boots, and knit cap pulled down over long, dirty-blonde hair, she looked like your run-of-the-mill Garrison County redneck.

"Morning," Stone said. "You his girlfriend or sister?"

"Girlfriend. I guess." She shrugged. "Sometimes, anyway."

"You just stood by and let him whip this horse?"

Another shrug. "He likes to hit things." She turned her head so he could see the bruise on her left cheek.

Stone clenched his jaw, staring at the angry, purple-and-yellow discoloration that marked her smooth skin. Then he turned around and stomped on the guy's left hand, feeling the bones collapse and crackle beneath his boot heel.

He turned back to the girl. "He won't be hitting you again anytime soon."

She tilted her head to the side like a quizzical puppy, giving him a look. "You're that sheriff-preacher, aren't you?"

Stone nodded.

She smiled crookedly. "You're not like any kind of preacher I've ever seen before."

"Yeah," Stone said. "I get that a lot."

———

Stone had hired a local contractor a few weeks back to build a barn and corral in the field behind the parsonage. He now leaned against one of the fence posts and listened to the sound of vehicles rumbling up his drive-way. Rocky stood behind him, breath pluming from his nostrils.

First came Holly in her Jeep Gladiator, followed closely by two SUVs, one bearing the logo of the High Peaks Animal Hospital from over in Ray Brook.

Holly approached Stone with a big smile on her face. "I brought the cavalry."

The doors of the unmarked SUV popped open and Lizzy stepped out, followed by a group of teenagers hauling first-aid gear. Lizzy pointed at Stone and said, "That's him."

"The high school has an elective veterinary science class," Holly explained. "Some of the kids wanted to help." She gestured at the Animal Hospital SUV where a middle-aged woman was climbing out from behind the wheel. "And as you can see, we brought Dr. Wray along too." She put a hand on Stone's arm. "Rocky is going to be well taken care of."

Stone patted her hand. "Thanks."

Holly quickly introduced the teenagers while the vet performed a basic checkup on a grudgingly cooperative Rocky. The students hovered around the horse, spoiling him with sugar cubes, apples, and carrots as they treated his wounds.

"Those cuts are nasty, but they're not infected, sheriff," one of the teenage boys, named Otter, said in passing. "We put some disinfectant on them. Probably leave some scars but he'll be okay."

"I reckon he's got some scars on the inside too," Stone said, reaching over and rubbing the stallion's neck. "We'll help him get past them."

"He's an awesome horse!" This from Abby, a short, slender girl with a nose ring. "Can we come out and visit him?"

"Sure," Stone said. "Anytime."

His thoughts turned inward, reflecting that he sometimes forgot that kindness still existed. He spent so much time staring into the face of evil that he often failed to remember that there were more good people out there than bad. These kids gave him hope. Hope for Rocky.

Hell, hope for himself. Hope that there was still a little light left in this too-often-dark world.

He gave the Appaloosa an affectionate pat, then moved to his back deck, sitting in one of the chairs. Holly joined him.

"Pretty amazing, huh?" She nudged him with an elbow. "These kids are really something."

"Sure are."

"Abby and Otter are brother and sister. They live on that farm just outside of Bloomingdale, across from the Red Canoe antique shop. Their mom breeds quarter horses. They both volunteer over at the Tri-Lakes Humane Society. They're good kids and I'm really glad Lizzy is friends with them."

They watched Abby walking Rocky around the corral, holding him by his halter. Lizzy kept pace alongside, watching carefully.

"Kind of weird to see a small girl like Abby wrangling horses," Holly said. "Not sure what her trick is, but she's a natural cowgirl. I think she just handles them like they're puppies."

Stone grinned. "Out in Texas, they say that having a horse around helps a girl get ready to deal with men when she's older."

"Oh, I seriously doubt Lizzy will have any problems with that," Holly said with a smile.

"You teaching her how to handle men?"

"I don't know about that. Given the fact that my ex-husband is a mobster, sometimes I'm not so sure I'm a good judge of men." Her eyes slid to Stone. "Other times, I'm pretty sure I know a good man when I see one."

Stone thought about all the things he had done and shook his head slightly. "Not sure I deserve to be called a good man."

Holly gave him a long, steady look with a faint,

mysterious glint in her eye that might mean something or might not mean anything at all. But instead of going further down that road, she changed the subject. "Any word from Agent Bester?"

"Not yet, but I'm sure I'll be hearing from her."

Holly asked, "She's a Supervisory Special Agent, right? Is that like a director or something? Is she some kind of big shot?"

"She probably has a corner office in the federal building down in Albany and probably runs a roster of at least fifty agents. Bester's a power player, no doubt."

"You don't resent that?"

"Resent what?"

"Her being more successful than you?"

"I don't want success," Stone said. "I just want peace and quiet."

"How's that working out for you?"

"It's a work in progress. By the way, Bester asked about you."

"What about?"

"Wanted to know if you were my girlfriend."

"What did you tell her?"

"The truth. She was happy to hear you're available."

"I'm only available to someone I want to be available to."

Stone looked at her. "She likes you. You know, that way."

"I know," Holly said, and left it at that.

———

When Stone pulled up at the sheriff's office later that afternoon, Deputy Drummond was waiting for him at the door with a wide smile on his face.

"Sheriff," the deputy said, "have I got a hell of a surprise for you."

"That a fact?" Stone hung up his rancher's coat and followed Drummond toward the holding cells in the back of the building.

"I was patrolling out by the Christmas tree farm this morning when I caught this guy thumbing for a ride."

There were four cells but only the first one was occupied. The man inside wore a red jacket, white cap, and blue jeans.

"Looks like we caught us another Yankee Doodle Dandy," Stone said.

NINETEEN

"EXPLAIN SOMETHING TO ME." Stone leaned against the cell bars and hooked his thumbs in his belt. "What's with all you guys dressing the same?"

Drummond had spent the last hour on the phone, and they now had a lot more information on the hitchhiker.

"What do you mean?" The guy's voice was thick and dull. He sounded exhausted and looked bleary-eyed. His whole demeanor was low-IQ, definitely not the sharpest knife in the drawer. "What other guys?"

The fact that this Yankee Doodle didn't know about the other ones caught Stone by surprise, but he didn't let it show.

"Your name is Frank," he said. "US Army. You're currently AWOL."

"Am not. I've got papers. They're in my duffel."

"They're forged. We checked with your base commander. They're sending out a couple of MPs to bring you back. But tell me what you know, and I'll put a good word in for you."

Frank just sat there, sullen and silent.

"C'mon, Frank. Who told you to dress like that?"

"Nobody."

"I'm not buying that bullshit. We dragged two dead guys out of ditches this week wearing the same exact clothes you are. They were both Army too, and they were both AWOL."

The corners of Frank's mouth twitched downward in a grimace, but he didn't say anything.

"There's a war going on," Stone said. "Truckers versus bikers. People are dying, Frank. If it was just scumbags killing scumbags, I'd probably just sit back and watch it happen. But innocent people are getting killed too. You need to help me stop this."

Frank still said nothing.

Stone smacked the bars with his palm. "What kind of soldier kills innocent people?"

"I didn't kill nobody!"

"You're not helping me stop them from getting killed," Stone shot back. "That's the same as deep-sixing them yourself."

Frank fidgeted for a few moments, shuffled his feet, and then sighed. "Fried pickles," he said.

"What?"

Frank looked up at him. "You got any fried pickles in this shithole town?"

"Yeah."

"Good. I'm starving. Get me some fried pickles and a Coke and I'll tell you what I know."

Stone sent Drummond over to the Jack Lumber for some "frickles" while he fetched a bottle of Coke from the break room fridge.

Thirty minutes later, Frank set the empty takeout container on his bunk, let out a belch just slightly less thunderous than the sound of a 747 crashing into the side of a mountain, and swiped the back of his hand across his mouth to get rid of the crumbs and ranch sauce.

"Feel better?" Stone asked.

Frank nodded. "Much."

"Good. Start talking."

"Okay, yeah. I'm a man of my word." Frank leaned back against the cement wall and folded his hands over his belly. "I was told that I was gonna be sent somewhere, on some kind of hush-hush assignment."

"Told by who?"

"He was a captain. He's the one who gave me those papers in my duffel bag. Said I was heading out on a mission and that I needed to follow my instructions exactly and not tell anyone, or else people could die."

"Tell me about the mission."

"I reported to an empty barracks room, and he was waiting. Told me to take off my uniform and put on the red, white, and blue clothes he gave me. Ordered me to leave the base and make my way to Garrison County where there were people waiting to pick me up and transport me to my destination."

"Where was that?"

"Bus station in Plattsburgh."

"He say who was going to transport you?"

"Guys in trucks. That's what the captain said. Told me once I reached Garrison County to just stay on the main roads and someone would stop for me. They would know to look for me because of the clothes."

"Tell me more about this captain."

"Not much to tell." Frank shrugged. "White guy. Fiftyish. Shaved head. Gray eyes."

"Any idea why he was sending you to the bus station in Plattsburgh?"

"I was supposed to pick up something out of the lockers. He gave me a key. It should be in my bag."

"What was in the locker?"

"Don't know. The captain never said. Just told me to

pick it up, put it in my backpack, and move it 'further up the road.' That's how he put it. Said it was like a relay race. One guy would take the package so far, drop it off, and wait for the next guy to pick it up and take it farther."

"Did he say why you had to wait?"

"Because the packages are too dangerous. At least, that's what the captain said. Move them slow, a little at a time. It's safer that way."

Back in his office, Stone dialed Bester's number. She answered on the second ring. "What's up, sheriff?"

"I've got a man dressed in red, white, and blue sitting in my lockup."

"I'm on my way."

"Make it quick. MPs are headed this way. Guy's AWOL."

"Shit!"

"Looks like he was involved in some sort of smuggling operation spearheaded by military personnel."

"Since it involves the military, we'll have to talk to CID."

"We also need to get to Plattsburgh ASAP."

"What's in Plattsburgh?"

"A bus locker."

"What's in the bus locker?"

"Not sure yet." Stone glanced at the key he'd fished out of Frank's backpack. "But I know how to find out."

Bester made some calls, pulled some strings, and got them access to the State Police helicopter out of Troop B.

The Bell 430 chopper boasted a cruising speed of 140 knots, or 161 mph, and would get them to Plattsburgh a whole lot faster than driving.

"Okay." Bester hung up and climbed into the Blazer. "They're firing the bird up now. I told them we'd be there in ten minutes."

"More like five," Stone said, pulling out of the station parking lot, hitting his lights and siren, and racing down Wildflower Avenue.

The roads were clear of snow and Stone was able to really floor it. Cars pulled over to the side as they approached, giving them a straight run. This time of year, darkness came early, and the light was already beginning to fade as they whipped past fields frosted with snow.

"Gonna be a night flight," Stone said.

"Doesn't bother me," Bester replied.

Two minutes later, they cut across the backside of Saranac Lake using McKenzie Pond Road and popped back out on the main drag in Ray Brook. Another half-minute and Stone pulled into the State Police headquarters and parked near the helipad where the Bell 430 waited to whisk them north. As he silenced his sirens, he could hear the mechanical roar of the steel bird.

During Stone's warrior days, he had ridden more helicopters than he cared to count, and one thing they had in common was that they all made an unholy racket. The rotor wash whipped snow from the edge of the helipad and sent it whirling into the dusk like little dust devils. Lights blinked and flashed along the chopper's fuselage.

Everything was wind and noise beneath the thrashing rotor blades. Stone ducked his chin, held onto his Stetson, and followed Bester to the door.

Inside, the cabin was warm, softly lit, and sound-proofed to reduce the engine noise. Bester grabbed a seat behind the pilot and pulled on her headset. Stone sat down and slipped on his own headset in time to hear her giving instructions to the pilot.

"...cleared to land at CVPH Medical Center. I've already called the Plattsburgh field office and they'll have a mobile unit and driver on standby there to take you to the bus station."

"Copy that." The pilot started toggling switches as Stone pulled the door shut. He could feel the thrumming vibrations as the chopper lifted off the pad.

Bester grinned at him. "This is it, Stone. You're about to get some answers on this case. Nice work."

"Just a lucky break. If Drummond hadn't come across another Yankee Doodle this morning, we still wouldn't know jackshit about what's going on."

Bester rubbed her hands together. "I can't wait to get a look at what's in that locker."

The Bell 430 rose into the darkening sky and banked north.

"Barf bags are right here." Bester thumped a seat pocket. "You know, in case the ride gets too rough for you."

"I've ridden in choppers before."

"Yeah, I figured you for an ex-service type." She smiled. "Maybe someday I'll pull your file and see who Lucas Stone was before he became a half-pastor, half-sheriff in the middle of nowhere."

Stone didn't bother telling her that there was no way in hell she would be able to access his records and if she even tried, she would receive strongly-worded phone calls from people way above her pay grade telling her to leave it alone...or else.

Bester gestured around the helicopter. "All this technology is putting your kind out of business."

"What kind is that?"

"Cowboys," she replied. "What you guys used to do

on horseback, they use choppers for now, right? For the big cattle drives?"

Stone nodded. "Choppers and ATVs, mostly. But there's still a need for men on horses in a cattle drive. Pretty sure there will always be a place for cowboys in this country."

"I beg to differ," Bester said. "I know it's a heartbreak for guys like you, but I think all that stuff is disappearing."

"What stuff?"

"All that old *man* stuff. Alpha male behavior, guy codes, macho bullshit, masculine rituals. The whole toxic, cowboy way of doing things."

"You're wrong. The cowboy way of life isn't going anywhere as long as there are men willing to live it."

Even as he spoke, Bester was shaking her head. "Face it, Stone, you're a dying breed. The days of the lone gunfighter facing down the bad guys are over. Say goodbye to the white male dream of domination."

"Domination? I mostly just dream about a good cup of coffee and a quiet evening at home."

"Explains why you don't have a girlfriend."

"Been poking into my private life?" Stone grinned. He appreciated that Bester was just busting his balls like any guy on the job would do, not trying to hide behind her femininity.

Bester said, "Poking your privates is the last thing I want to do, Stone, believe me," and they both had a good laugh.

A short time later, Plattsburgh materialized below them, the city lights gleaming like a puddle of glowing jewels in the darkness. The pilot switched on his landing lights. A halogen beam spotlighted the helipad of the Champlain Valley Medical Center as the chopper began its descent.

"I've got a driver waiting and the bus station is cordoned off," Bester said.

"Bomb squad?" Stone suggested, since they had no idea what they were going to find in that locker.

"Already on standby."

"Good call."

The chopper set down on the hospital rooftop with a surprisingly gentle bump. Stone opened the door and Bester followed him out, dumping her headset on the vacated seat behind her.

They took an elevator down to the street, leaving behind the *whump-whump-whump* roar of the rotor blades. A Bureau SUV waited for them at the curb, engine warm, ready to go.

Stone could feel the adrenaline starting to pulse through him as they climbed into the vehicle. He didn't know what would happen next, but he was ready.

"Bus station," Bester ordered the driver. "Lights and sirens and I don't want to see your foot anywhere near the brake pedal."

TWENTY

THE SUV RACED down Route 9, headlights punching through the darkness while the emergency lights pulsed an electronic rhythm.

When Bester spoke, her words surprised Stone.

"So you're a preacher."

"Last time I checked."

"Bible in one hand, gun in the other. You don't find that to be a conflict of interest?"

"I have plenty of conflicts," Stone replied. "But being a preacher and being a sheriff isn't one of them."

Bester seemed to hesitate for a moment, then said, "Stone, do you believe God is real?"

Stone recognized that they were crossing into personal rather than professional territory. "Yeah, I do."

She looked at him. "Not sure I do. I've seen things that shouldn't have happened if God is really up there."

So that's what was troubling her. That age-old question: *If there is a God, how can He allow evil to exist?*

No doubt she had seen things, terrible things, as a federal agent. She dealt with criminal profiling, which meant she came across the worst of the worst. She had seen the bloody aftermaths of murder-suicides, the charnel house slaughter of mass shootings, the burnt, blackened victims of arsonists and bombers. She had seen innocent children abducted, violated, tortured, and butchered.

Stone knew from personal experience that if you weren't careful, that sort of darkness seeped into your head and stayed there, giving birth to all kinds of doubts and demons.

Bester projected her toughness like a straight-edge razor. But sometimes even the toughest aren't immune to the poisoning of the soul that comes from spending too many years with death and destruction as close acquaintances.

"Tell me what's bothering you," Stone said.

Bester was quiet for a long time before she finally spoke.

"Our jobs. The things we do. The violence we so often have to resort to. I killed a man last year with my bare hands. Crushed his windpipe. He was trying to kill me and had knocked my weapon away, so I had every legal right to defend myself. I went through the usual. Administrative leave, the investigation…you know."

"The killing was ruled justified, I take it?"

"Yeah."

"But you're not okay with it?"

"I did what I had to do. But…" She sighed. "I'm just not sure anymore that we're always on the side of the angels."

"Sometimes we are, sometimes we aren't," Stone said. "Nobody's perfect. But one thing I know for sure: choking the shit out of some bastard who was trying to kill you isn't wrong. Where I come from, we call that justice."

"Yeah, I suppose. I think maybe the stress of being an SSA just gets to me sometimes."

Stone respected her honesty but before he could respond, the driver pulled up in front of the bus station. The place had been cleared out and cordoned off with yellow tape. Plattsburgh Police Department personnel were on site, diverting traffic, controlling the scene, and making sure nobody got anywhere near the terminal.

Stone and Bester exited the SUV and headed for the main doors. Once inside, they spotted rows of orange lockers tucked up against a wall. He dug into his pocket and pulled out the key. "We're looking for locker number thirty-eight."

They quickly scanned the lockers and found #38 at the end of the third row. Stone slid the key in the lock and twisted. The door opened.

Inside the locker was a suitcase, a hard-shell number sitting upright on its wheels with the extendable handle recessed.

"Bingo." Bester signaled to the bomb squad and then she and Stone withdrew. The bomb boys would make sure the luggage wasn't wired to blow if moved or tilted before they fished it out for further investigation.

Stone left Bester leaning against the SUV and hiked up the street to a convenience store for some coffee. When he got back, Bester was sending a text.

"Thanks," she said, accepting the steaming Styrofoam cup he offered her. She took a sip, glanced at the screen again, and then abruptly pocketed the phone.

"Everything all right?" Stone asked.

Bester let out a bitter laugh. "No, everything is not all right," she replied. "But I'm not talking to a preacher about it."

"I take it you had some bad experiences with preachers in the past."

"Let's just say men of God don't tend to be over sympathetic to women of my sexual orientation."

"That's their problem." Stone sipped his coffee and watched the bomb squad work through the glass front wall of the bus station. "The one thing we know for sure about God is that He accepts us. There's a whole lot of gay-bashing preachers out there who conveniently forget that."

"That's a refreshingly different take on the subject."

"Christ told us to come as we are." Stone shrugged. "Preachers can make exceptions if they want to, but I don't think God does. Seems pretty simple and clear cut to me."

"I think I'd probably like your church," Bester said.

"You're welcome anytime. You and…"

"Pauline." Bester crossed her arms as she said the name. "We've been together eight years."

"Good for you."

"Sure you don't want to rain fire and brimstone down on my head?"

"Sorry, but you'll get no condemnation from me." He paused to take a drink. Even bundled up, it was freezing cold out here, and the hot coffee helped ward off the chill. "But I get the impression things aren't going well. You seem preoccupied and I definitely noticed the look you gave Holly."

Bester smiled. "You saw that, huh?"

"Hard to miss. But it's not the look of someone who is happy in their current relationship. Something wrong between you and Pauline?"

"You're very perceptive."

"Not trying to intrude if you don't want to talk about it."

"No, you're fine, Stone." Bester sighed. "Like I said, Pauline and I have been together eight years. She says that's long enough and that it's time for us to make it permanent."

"And you're not ready."

"I didn't have much of a youth." Bester stared off into the night. "I went from high school to Annapolis, to the Navy. From there to the FBI. Once I got in the Bureau, I focused on climbing the ladder, making it all the way to SAS. It's been a busy life and it didn't leave me time to have much fun. You ever feel that way, Stone? Like your life is half over and you haven't even begun to enjoy it yet?" She tapped the plastic lid of her coffee cup. "I don't want to die before I get the chance to feel alive again."

Before Stone could reply, the bomb squad gave them the thumbs up, letting them know they were cleared to come back in. Bester and Stone hustled back into the terminal. The suitcase lay open beside the locker.

"Well, it's not a bomb," Bester said as she walked over and looked down at the carefully-opened luggage.

"No," Stone said. "It's worse."

He recognized the packages of C-4 plastic explosive, all of them marked with US ARMY stencilling. Looked like two dozen all together, neatly stacked like bricks of clay in their individual wrappers. Two boxes of detonators were stored in the suitcase's front pocket.

"Good God." Bester whistled, low and ominous. "There's enough here to start a war."

TWENTY-ONE

"HOW MANY YANKEE Doodles have there been?"

Bester shook her head. "I don't even want to think about how many bus station lockers have—or had—suitcases full of C-4. Could be a dozen, could be a hundred... who knows? What we do know is this: somebody's been stealing and trafficking US military explosives. We've stumbled onto something big."

"Like stepping on a snake," Stone said. "Problem is, now we have to figure out how to step off and kill it without getting bit first."

After the chopper ride back to Whisper Falls, they had reconvened at the sheriff's office. They were joined by Jim Spencer from the State Police. Stone knew Drummond and Valentine were probably hovering outside his door, hoping to overhear something.

"Near as we can tell," said Bester, "it's being coordinated from inside the Army, so CID will have to be involved."

"This is going to be a cross-jurisdictional mess," Spencer replied. "Far as the State Police are concerned, you feds can take lead on this one."

"This will be a federal show," Bester assured him. "FBI on point, probably coordinating with DHS and God knows how many other alphabet agencies."

Stone knew what that meant. The Garrison County Sheriff's Department was out of the game.

He and his deputies had played their part. Yeah, he still had Dorey and the Attorney General's audit to deal with, but the burden of the main investigation had shifted. This was no longer a local murder and missing person case; it was a skein in a nationwide thread, with national security repercussions. It required the reach and resources of the federal government, far beyond what some rural county sheriff could provide.

As the meeting progressed, Stone tuned out. He had come to Whisper Falls to escape this kind of large-scale threat and the violence that almost inevitably accompanied it, because it took more than prayers to combat evil – it took copious amounts of firepower. Terrorists and their ilk were mad dogs and sometimes the only way to put down a mad dog was a bullet in the head.

He had come here for the quiet of small-town life. He knew you couldn't run from the demons of your past, but you could give them less fuel to feed on. So instead of listening to Bester lay out the plan of attack to deal with this threat, he thought about the so-called small things that mattered most to him. Holly, Lizzy, Max, Rocky, his church...and the memory of Jasmine, the daughter he had lost but who would still be with him forever.

Yeah, he had done his time in the big leagues. Let someone else fight the dirty wars. After what he had done to the child-killing survivalists last year, he couldn't exactly say his warrior days were over, but now he only wanted to use those lethal skills to protect his little corner of the world.

Bester was still talking. "...stage up for now at the FBI

field office in Plattsburgh. Stone, on behalf of the Bureau, let me say thanks for all the help you and your deputies provided on this."

"Yeah, fantastic job, Stone," Spencer seconded. "We appreciate everything you guys did."

"Give me a call if you need anything," Stone said. "You know, like if you need me to fix a speeding ticket for you or something."

When the meeting ended, Stone walked Bester out to her Range Rover.

"It was good working with you, Stone." He could sense the sincerity in her voice. "You're a good sheriff, a good preacher, and just a damn good man."

"I don't know about all that," Stone said. "But I try my best and that's all a man can do."

Bester put her hands on her hips and looked down Main Street, all lit up after dark. Some of the storefronts still had Christmas lights blinking in their windows.

"This is a nice little town," she commented. "Pauline would like it here. Maybe we'll come visit." She smiled. "You know, in the summer, when it's not so cold that the air hurts my face."

"You'd both be welcome anytime," Stone replied.

"Thanks." She smiled and for once there was no cynical or bitter edge to it. "Never figured an alpha male cowboy like you would turn out to be a nice guy."

"I'll try to be more of a mean son of a bitch next time you see me," Stone said with a little grin.

Bester chuckled. "It really was good meeting you, Stone." She gave him a wink. "Say goodbye to Holly for me."

"I'll do that."

She reached out and touched his arm, gave him a warm smile, and then drove away. Stone watched her taillights recede into the night, heading back to the concrete jungle she called home. Some people thrived in the city, but he wasn't one of them. Give him the mountains, the fresh air, the vast expanse of open skies. There was a reason he lived in a place like Whisper Falls.

He climbed into his Blazer thinking that he couldn't wait for things to get back to normal.

TWENTY-TWO

THREE DAYS LATER, Stone sat astride Rocky on an open knoll beside a brook, the water somewhat brackish green from having flowed through a swampy wetland a half-mile back. He was trying to keep his emotions from descending into full-on melancholy, but there was no denying he was in a brooding mood.

He had always done some of his best thinking on a horse. It had been a long time – too long – since he had ridden.

Not since Texas, he thought.

His hand drifted up to the snakeskin band that circled the crown of his Stetson.

Jasmine had been the innocent age of seven when the diamondback rattler spooked her horse, and she was thrown from the saddle and killed. He had killed the snake and buried his daughter and tried to move on, but the despair he felt at losing his only child had exerted a soul-twisting effect on his life, deflecting him onto a dark detour that lasted for years.

It was a darkness that he knew still existed within him.

Rocky stamped and shifted beneath him, swaying slightly in the cool air of the early afternoon.

Stone leaned forward and patted the stallion's neck. "We're just a couple of survivors, aren't we?" The horse whinnied softly in response. Stone's cowboy senses told him that he and the stallion were going to get along just fine.

His thoughts turned to the Dorey investigation.

The court had ruled the case would go forward. Despite Slidell's slime-ball maneuver of demanding an AG audit of the Garrison County Sheriff's Department, Dorey remained locked up. The evidence was still thin, but Stone had assigned Valentine to dig further, starting with Cardine Trucking.

While the prosecutor accessed state employment records to track down the home addresses of Cardine's employees so subpoenas could be issued, Valentine would go through the company's buildings in Milford with the proverbial fine-tooth comb. The young deputy might carry a minor chip on his shoulder due to his youth and getting teased about his romantic last name, but he was damn persistent when given an assignment. If there was anything to be found at Cardine, he would find it.

Stone stared at the water rippling over the smooth, rounded rocks in the brook. The larger ones jutted up out of the water, their tops crested with snow like a dollop of whipped cream. There was serenity in the murmuring song of the stream and the quiet of the woods, but not enough to keep the foreboding at bay.

Just before saddling up, he'd received the unwelcome news that Homer Pressfield, his fellow preacher and extremism expert, was in the hospital. Details were sparse, but it sounded like Homer had suffered something terrible and violent. Given everything that was going on around here, Stone seriously doubted it was an accident.

A sharp, piercing cry from above pulled his gaze skyward. He looked up to see the dark figure of a hawk circling like a predatory shadow.

He pulled his coat tighter around his frame, even though the chill he felt had nothing to do with the cold air. He couldn't shake the feeling that something was coming. Something was closing in on Whisper Falls. Something dark and formless, like a winter storm at dusk.

He believed in heaven, but it felt like hell was riding his way.

———

"Ready?" Holly asked as Stone slid into the passenger seat of her Jeep Gladiator. She waited for him to fasten his seatbelt and then handed him a glass casserole dish covered with tinfoil.

"What's this?"

"It's for the potluck the parents are putting on." Holly pulled out of Stone's driveway and headed for town.

"Who's bringing the beer?"

"It's a high school art show, Luke. No alcohol allowed on the premises."

"Right. That just means one of the students will bring it."

Holly rolled her eyes. "Cynical much?"

"Only right before art shows."

"Lizzy will be happy you tagged along. She likes it when we spend time together." Holly gave him a side-long smile. "She really likes you, Luke."

"I like her too. She's a good kid. Just like her mom."

"Except I'm not a kid anymore."

"Well, I didn't want to say anything, but now that you mention it..."

"Jerk," Holly said, but with a warm smile.

Whisper Falls High School was an imposing old brick building built like a cube, but the interior had been renovated back in the late '90s thanks to a state grant to modernize the classrooms and labs. Tonight's event was being held in the larger of the school's two gymnasiums.

"You won't believe Lizzy's sculpture," Holly said. They parked and proceeded across the lot toward the well-lit entrance. "It's life-size."

"A sculpture? What'd she use, stone or wood?"

"Paper mâché," Holly replied.

"Impressive."

Lizzy greeted them just inside the doors, her friend Abby beside her. Both were dressed in a kind of hip, late bohemian style that was out of place in this small mountain town, but for a couple of teenage girls, that was probably the point. They were both clearly excited.

"Luke, it's so cool that you're here." Lizzy gave his arm a quick squeeze. "What's in the dish?"

"Casserole," Holly answered. "And no, Luke didn't make it."

"We can all thank God for that," Stone said. It was a joke because he was actually a halfway decent cook.

Holly took the dish out of his hands and glanced around the school lobby. "Does this place have a kitchen?"

"This way." Lizzy headed down a long, cavernous hallway and Holly followed, leaving Stone alone with Abby.

"Come on." Abby's nose ring glittered under the fluorescent lights as she spun around in a half-pirouette, her heavy combat boots making her clumsy. "I'll give you a personal, guided tour of the artwork."

"Lead the way," Stone said. Clearly Abby was a little bit goth, a little bit punk, which explained why she and Lizzy were friends. They both marched to their own drumbeats, and he admired that.

"For a small town, we've got more artists than you might think." Abby paused by a large, framed canvas that must have been at least six feet tall and two feet wide. Depicted against the white background was a huge semicolon, as if left there by a typewriter the size of a bulldozer.

"Does it have a name?" Stone asked.

"Yeah. 'Orthography.'" She said it quickly, as if she wanted to get it out of the way and move on to something else. She seemed to have the kind of brain where thoughts ricocheted rapidly from one subject to the next like a manic pinball, with zero pause and little segue. "Luke, can I ask you a question?" She didn't wait for permission. "Does being a sheriff with the last name 'Stone' ever cause trouble when you're dealing with druggies?"

"It hasn't so far."

"Like the Bob Dylan song." Abby was on the move again, shuffling over to the next display. "About how everybody must get stoned."

"Not exactly your era of music," Stone said. "I'm guessing you overheard your dad playing it."

"Stepdad," Abby corrected. "And yeah, he turned me and Stanley onto that record years ago."

"Stanley? I thought your brother's name was Otter."

"It is. We call him Otter or Stanley." Abby stopped at the next piece, which happened to be Lizzy's.

Stone thought it looked pretty damn amazing.

Although its surface was a bit rough and rumpled and some of the finer details blurry due to the medium, the paper mâché sculpture was clearly identifiable as a centaur – part human, part horse. Lizzy had created a young boy centaur of maybe seven or eight years old. The look of innocence on the boy's face was remarkably lifelike.

"Isn't he cool?" Abby enthused. "Lizzy calls him Avalon. I just call him Fred."

"Why?"

Abby shrugged. "I call everybody that. It's easier than remembering everyone's name."

"Doesn't that get confusing when you're with a bunch of friends?"

"Nah. Otter's usually there to translate for me."

As if summoned by the mention of his name, Otter appeared, dragging a man along behind him. A large, bear-shaped man with a beard and long hair wearing combat boots—like stepfather, like daughter—and an ill-fitting blazer.

At the same moment, Holly touched his arm. "Enjoying the tour?"

"Sure am. Abby told me Otter's real name is Stanley. Didn't you say his stepdad was a member of…?"

"Hey, Sonny!" Abby called loudly, apparently one of those kids who referred to their stepfather by their first name. She waved, gesturing him and Otter over.

When they got closer, Stone locked eyes with one of the Children.

TWENTY-THREE

STONE RECOGNIZED Sonny from that day at Blaine's Billiards. And Sonny clearly recognized him too.

Otter made the formal introductions. "Sheriff Stone, this is our stepdad, Sonny."

The two men met each other's gaze coolly, the lawman and the biker having a stare down in the middle of a school gym like two old west gunslingers squaring off. Left with no choice but to be civilized, they shook hands briefly, gave each other curt nods, and stepped back.

Holly was too busy gazing around at the artwork to pick up on the hostile vibes. "Isn't this incredible?" she said. "All this great stuff by our kids. Otter, where's yours?"

"Over here. C'mon, I'll show you. It's supercool." Otter tugged her sleeve and she and Abby followed him through the maze of displays. Stone and Sonny were left standing awkwardly together in front of a paper mâché centaur.

"You were at Blaine's the other day," Sonny said, his tone conversational rather than adversarial. "I thought you were about to catch an ass whooping, but I should have known Roy's too smart for that."

"How about the rest of you?"

Sonny smiled, revealing chipped teeth. "We ride together, boss, but that don't mean we all think alike." Sonny jerked a thumb over his shoulder, back toward the school entrance. "Come on outside with me while I have a smoke."

Impelled more by curiosity than anything, Stone followed the biker outside and down a walkway to a bench nestled among a frozen flowerbed. Sonny brushed off the snow, took a seat, and fired up a Marlboro. Stone stayed standing.

"I'm going to tell you some things, sheriff," Sonny said quietly. "But you didn't hear it from me, okay? We never met, we never talked. You understand the rules of this little chat?"

"Not my first confidentiality rodeo," Stone replied. "Give it to me straight. It won't come back to you."

"You were asking about the trucks, about the beef between the Children and Cardine. Truth is I don't know what's going on myself. Not many of us do."

"Fair enough," Stone said. "I'll take you at your word…for now."

Sonny sucked in a lungful of carcinogens and exhaled them in twin plumes of smoke through his nostrils. "I've lived hard, and ridden hard, my whole life. But Abby and Otter and their mom are the best thing ever happened to me. It'd kill me to see something bad happen to them."

"Why would anything bad happen to them?"

Sonny took another drag on his cigarette, the tip glowing orange in the night. It reminded Stone of a sentry he had killed outside a bioweapons research facility in China toward the tail end of his warrior days.

That bullet had split the sentry's cigarette right down the middle before doing the same thing to his skull.

"It's like this," Sonny said. "Once upon a time we did some business with Cardine. This was years back, right after Roy took over the club. I took a drive out there with Roy twice to pick up some boxes." He held up a hand when Stone started to say something. "Don't ask me what was in them 'cause I got no idea. Roy said he just wanted me there for backup. But I saw that Roy and the owner, a guy named Rohmer, they knew each other. Like, not just business associates, but *friends*."

"There's no law against that."

"Yeah, well, there should be a law against friends like Rohmer." Sonny dropped the spent cigarette, ground it underfoot, and immediately fired up another one. "After the second visit, on the way back, I asked Roy about Rohmer. Sheriff, let me tell you what, that guy's one bad dude."

"What makes you say that?"

Sonny seemed unsettled. Stone wondered what kind of man Rohmer had to be to make a member of the Children uneasy.

The biker finally spoke again. "You know, most so-called bad men in this world also have a good side. Like, a guy might sell drugs but always shows up for his daughter's soccer games. The bank robber who donates half his take to the church. The hitman who visits his mom in the nursing home. Bad men, but they've got a streak of good in them. You know what I mean?"

"I suppose," Stone allowed.

"Yeah, well, Rohmer doesn't have that good streak," Sonny said. "He's one of those guys with a snake soul who brings evil with him wherever he goes. Like, literally evil. He and Roy were both involved in the occult scene."

"Not exactly your run-of-the-mill bad guys then," Stone said.

"Roy's not involved in that crap anymore. Or so he says, at least. But for a short period he was into it big-time. He was reading all sorts of weird books and even joined an occult study group over in Burlington. But the more Roy got to know Rohmer, the more he realized that Rohmer was into some really dark stuff, like full-bore Satanism. Not the stupid stuff you see on TV, but the serious shit."

"So something more than just upside down crosses and inverted pentagrams."

"Right. Way worse than that." Sonny shook his head. "We're talking about weapons-trafficking, sex-trafficking, white slavery. Murder. The kind of people who celebrate school shootings and look to sow violence and mayhem wherever they can. That's the kind of guy Rohmer is."

"Sounds like one sick son of a bitch."

"You better believe it. Roy's a hard guy, tough as nails. But Rohmer was too far gone even for Roy. He got spooked and we stopped making trips to Cardine to see Rohmer. A few months later, you've got a trucker-biker war going down with a side order of dead hitchhikers. What's it all mean?" Sonny shrugged. "Hell if I know. But I thought *you* should know, sheriff."

"Sounds like Rohmer took it personal when Roy walked away from him."

Sonny's second cigarette was almost gone. He took one last drag and flicked it into a snowbank as he said, "It's like a lover's quarrel gone deadly."

"I appreciate you telling me this," Stone said. "And you have my word that I'll keep it confidential. I can't tell you everything about the investigation but I will tell you this much. I went up to Cardine with an FBI agent. Rohmer pulled a gun on us. We went back the next day and he had disappeared, the whole company cleared out. Everything gone. So yeah, something about Rohmer just isn't right. Your background info helps put some of the puzzle together."

"Glad I could help." Sonny stood up. "I think two cigarettes is enough. What do you say we head back inside and find some food?"

"Sounds good."

They walked back to the school, joining the growing crowd of art show visitors.

"You kind of have to wonder," Sonny said. "Cardine had a pretty big fleet. At least fifteen, twenty trucks."

"Yeah?" Stone glanced at him. "So?"

"Where the hell did they all go?"

It was a good question, Stone had to admit. There were a couple people he could ask: Dorey, except that Slidell was blocking that avenue; or Hauser, if he ever regained consciousness. It was a thread worth following because Sonny was right – Rohmer's ability to fold up his tent and vanish into the night without a trace was impressive.

Almost like he cut a deal with the devil, Stone thought bemusedly as he searched for Holly among the exhibits.

He caught sight of her and noted the look of relief on her face when their eyes met. It took him a moment to realize that the man standing beside her with his back turned was Scott Slidell. He made his way over, realizing that Holly needed rescuing.

"Ah, good evening, sheriff." Slidell turned around as Stone approached. "I did not take you for a patron of the arts."

Stone gave him a cool look as he stepped up beside Holly and instinctively slid his arm around her waist. He hoped she wouldn't blow the play by pulling away and giving Slidell an opening.

Instead, she pressed up against him, warm and natural, and hooked an arm around his waist. Stone was not a man who lied to himself much and he had to admit it felt good.

"My sister invited me." Slidell seemed compelled to offer an explanation for his presence. "She's one of the guidance counselors."

"So maybe you should go hang out with her," Stone said flatly.

"Why, sheriff, it's almost as if you're trying to get rid of me."

"You think?" Holly muttered under her breath so that only Stone heard her.

Stone made a show of checking his watch. "Time for us to go take another look at Lizzy's centaur. Lead the way, Holly."

"The centaur? That's your daughter's?" Slidell seemed genuinely surprised. "It's excellent work! Truly stunning. One of the best pieces in the show."

"Thanks, Scott. I'll let her know you said that," Holly replied.

"Please do. You two have a nice evening." Slidell started to turn away, then swiveled back around. "Oh, sheriff, by the way..."

Stone gritted his teeth. "What is it, Scott?"

"Thought you might want to know. I just got the text a few minutes ago." He paused for dramatic effect. "Mr. Hauser died in the hospital an hour ago."

TWENTY-FOUR

"WE DID ALL WE COULD," the doctor at Adirondack Medical Center said the next morning. "Mr. Hauser's head injuries resulted in a brain bleed. We operated and gave it our best shot, but it was too late."

Stone felt a weight pressing down on him. He had dealt with plenty of death in his years, a lot of it caused by his direct actions. It got easier, but it never got easy, and that was probably the way it should be.

He asked if the family had made arrangements.

"All taken care of." The doctor looked at Stone. "I understand you're a preacher as well as a sheriff. I'm a believer myself. Times like this, all we can do is pray."

"Say a prayer for the ones left behind. It's all we can do."

They sat in silence for a few heartbeats, each with their own thoughts. Then the doctor brightened. "By the way, got a friend of yours here. Another preacher. Homer Pressfield."

That caught Stone by surprise. "Figured he was at the hospital in Plattsburgh."

The doctor shook his head. "The incident happened down in Keene Valley, so they brought him here."

"What happened?"

"You should probably ask him that yourself."

Stone took the elevator to the second floor of the hospital and found Homer Pressfield in the last room at the end of the corridor, right next to the stairs and as far away from the nurse's station as you could get. His window looked out over Lake Colby on the other side of the road, a scattering of ice fishing shacks dotting the frozen water.

Pressfield lay in the bed watching a morning talk show on TV, half his head swaddled in bandages. Despite his injuries, he cracked a smile when Stone walked into the room.

"How's it going?" Stone asked as he sat down in one of the chairs.

"As you can see, I've been better." Pressfield chuckled. "Do me a favor and turn off the TV so we can talk."

Stone grabbed the remote and muted the television. "You look pretty banged up, brother. What happened?"

Pressfield sighed. "It began last week." His voice sounded weak, a far cry from the confident orator who had spoken at Stone's church. "I started receiving notes. Anonymous envelopes through the door slot, in my mailbox, left on my car windshield, that sort of thing. They were like those ransom notes in movies where they cut out words and letters from the newspaper. One said, 'Watch your mouth or you'll meet God face to face' and another one said 'The Remnant is watching.'"

Stone felt his blood turn cold.

The Remnant is watching...

He gestured at the bandage half-mummifying

Homer's head. "Apparently they escalated from cheap threats to actual violence."

Pressfield nodded. "I had just finished speaking at a church down in Schroon Lake. On the way back home, I decided to stop at the Noon Mark Diner for a late dinner. They hit me on that long stretch just outside the village, next to that grass airstrip. This black SUV just swerved right out in front of me. I slammed the brakes so hard I banged my head on the steering wheel. Next thing I know, someone yanked open the door and dragged me out of the car. They threw me on the ground and beat the snot out of me. Never felt anything like it. Fists. Boots. Some sort of club. I thought they were going to kill me."

Rage flowed through Stone's veins like liquid fire. If the scumbags who had done this to Homer had been here right now, he would have gladly ripped their throats out with his bare hands. Pressfield was a good man, but more than that, a *gentle* man. He wasn't a warrior or a fighter, which made his beat down all the more unfair.

"I tried to crawl away," Pressfield continued, "but there were too many of them. I just laid there and took the beating."

"Sometimes that's all you can do," Stone said.

"When I regained consciousness, I was here in the hospital." He looked at Stone with frightened eyes. "Luke, between the threatening letters and this attack, I think it's safe to say that The Remnant is on the move. You have to stop them."

———

The Remnant is on the move...

The rage uncoiled within Stone once again, writhing like a nest of black vipers deep down where the dark impulses dwell. A glance in the rear view mirror as he drove back to Whisper Falls showed the unholy glare in his eyes.

Homer Pressfield was a good man, one of the best Stone had ever met, a lifelong preacher who had baptized, blessed, and buried thousands of people over the course of his ministry. You would be hard-pressed to find a more humble, hardworking servant of God.

Yet those bastards beat him in the middle of the road like a goddamned dog.

Stone fought to control his anger as he cruised into town. A light snow drifted down from a cloud-choked sky, a scattering of dandruff-like flakes, nothing worth calling out the plow trucks over.

Stone believed in justice. Sometimes legal, but sometimes primal. Vulnerable victims deserved justice when preyed upon by vicious predators. Those too weak to fight for themselves deserved someone to fight for them. God had put warriors on this earth for just that reason and Stone knew, despite the doubts that sometimes weighed down his soul, that he was such a man.

He simply refused to stand idle while evil flourished. He had been a man of war before becoming a man of God and he often found himself trying to balance between the seemingly polar opposite ends of the spectrum. He could pray and comfort and minister one moment, then turn around and cold-bloodedly kill the next. Whatever light lurked inside him was not enough to drive out the darkness, the belief that sometimes justice came at the end of a bullet.

A Bible in one hand, a gun in the other. That was his life.

Stone looped around to the eastern outskirts of town and turned into the trailer park there. Not much of a park really, since there were only four trailers, but Stone figured it wasn't worth splitting hairs over. He pulled into the lot occupied by Deputy Drummond's house-on-wheels and parked the Blazer.

"Sheriff!" On his day off, the department's longest-serving deputy greeted Stone wearing a fuzzy green bathrobe, slippers that looked like moccasins, and holding a longhaired white cat in his arms. "Well, this is a surprise. I wasn't expecting visitors."

"Sorry to bother you, Doug. Mind if I come in?"

"Sure thing." Drummond opened the door wider and gestured at the couch. "Have a seat."

Drummond had been the first deputy to throw his support behind Stone when he took over as sheriff. The boss-subordinate nature of their relationship meant they weren't really friends, but Stone respected the man. Drummond was a damn good deputy, a patient, experienced cop with a steady work ethic that lightened everyone's load. Stone had never once heard him complain about an assignment.

He quickly sketched out what had happened to Homer Pressfield, then said, "When you come back to work, I need you to coordinate with the other police departments in the tri-lakes area. Make sure they know we think The Remnant is messing around in our backyard."

Drummond let out a low whistle. "The Remnant are bad news, boss. Not your garden-variety yahoos or gun nuts. Not by a long shot."

"I know. And now that they're ramping up the violence around these parts, we need to coordinate with the other departments so we're all ready for them." Stone still couldn't shake the nebulous feeling that something was closing in on the town and he didn't like it, not one damn bit.

"Sure, no problem," Drummond said. "Want me to put Valentine on this too?"

"I've got Cade working the Cardine Trucking angle. Let him focus on that for now unless you need another set of hands."

Drummond nodded. The cat slipped from his lap as he picked up a notebook and wandered over to sniff Stone's boots. Then the creature looked up at Stone as if to say, *Mind if I jump up there and join you?*

"Careful, sheriff." Drummond chuckled. "Ol' Barney there will do his damnedest to make you his best friend if you let him."

Stone wasn't much of a cat person. He gave Barney a warning glare that let the cat know his affections wouldn't be appreciated. Barney blinked slowly, clearly unimpressed. As the sole companion to a middle-aged widower, the cat was undoubtedly accustomed to getting his own way.

Drummond had found a pen and was scribbling in the notebook. "I'll get on the horn first thing tomorrow morning. I'll start with Saranac Lake PD, see what they have for profiles on Remnant members, then work the phones to the other departments in the area."

"Sounds good," Stone said. "I'll call Bester and see if the FBI has any info they can share with us." Stone looked down as Barney started rubbing against his pant leg, purring loud enough to drown out a chainsaw.

"Looks like you made a friend." Drummond grinned. "Did you have a favorite cat growing up?"

"Sure did."

"What was its name?"

"Roadkill."

TWENTY-FIVE

"OKAY," said Mason. "Let's see where we're at..."

As the prosecutor sorted through a mountain of folders on his desk, Stone studied the room around him. Mason's office resembled a garbage dump. A half dozen open briefcases spilled files across the conference table and floor. Stacks of books, some open, covered nearly every available surface and a pyramid of file boxes in the corner nearly reached the ceiling. The guy was clearly a packrat. It was amazing he could locate anything in this mess.

"Found it! Okay." Mason settled his reading glasses on the bridge of his nose, leaned back in his chair, and cracked open a folder. "Our strategy is to show there's a conspiracy involved in the attack on the dead biker. Shooting straight with you, sheriff, I have to say that evidence is pretty thin."

Stone gave him a sour look.

"I dug into their employment records and subpoenaed some of their drivers to submit to a deposition." Mason shrugged. "So far, no joy. Seems all the drivers we've tried to contact have all bugged out. A lot of frustrated landlords talking about properties abandoned and rent left unpaid." He made a *not-much-we-can-do* gesture with his hands. "The truckers have gone to ground. Hard to get evidence from ghosts."

Stone frowned. "The fact that all the drivers have disappeared must raise some red flags."

"It's suspicious, sure, but it's also circumstantial."

"What about Rohmer, the owner?"

"He's AWOL too." Mason closed the file and tossed it on his desk. "Any news on the AG's audit of your department?"

"Haven't heard anything yet."

"You won't, not any time soon. They're swamped." Mason sighed. "Clever tactic on Slidell's part. He knows we might get a conviction but if the AG finds something during the audit, he can bring it up during the appeal."

Stone tried not to feel frustrated. Slidell was a thorn in his side, but he was low priority. There were more important things to focus on than a bottom-feeding defense attorney.

"We still have some time," Mason said. "Not long, though. Trial begins in a few days. Unless you want me to file a motion for continuance?"

"Not yet. I've got Valentine nosing around Cardine Trucking. Maybe he'll turn up something. Or maybe you'll track down one of the truckers and beat a confession out of them."

"Sure, maybe." Mason's tone made it clear he thought they had a better chance of seeing a kamikaze squadron of flying pigs.

Deputy Cade Valentine was slightly – okay, *more* than slightly – annoyed with his assignment this morning.

Everyone knew that Cardine Trucking was a dead end. The truckers had bugged out for parts unknown and left the place stripped clean like a vulture-picked carcass. But since he was running out of leads, Stone wanted it double-checked, so he pawned it off on the department rookie.

Valentine didn't despise Stone like he had Grant Camden, the previous – and now deceased – sheriff, but he didn't really care for him much either. It was just bred into him. Born and raised in the close-knit community of Whisper Falls, Valentine had a natural distrust of outsiders who came to town, especially ones who ended up staking down roots. Far as he was concerned, Drummond, as the senior deputy, should have been the interim sheriff. Not that the old-timer seemed to want the job, but still, it shouldn't have gone to an outsider like Stone.

Valentine conducted a half-hearted search of the trucking facility and found nothing. He stood in the truck bay, which still smelled of oil and diesel, and tried to decide if he wanted to waste any more time here.

Finally he said, "Screw this," and headed back to his police cruiser. He hadn't been gone long; the coffee he'd bought at the diner up the road was still warm. Yeah, it had been a half-assed search all right. But it had been a wild goose chase from the start, so he didn't feel that guilty about cutting it short. What's the worst thing Stone could do about it? Yell at him? He'd been chewed out before.

He took Route 374 East out of Milford until it connected with Route 3, then pointed the squad car back toward Whisper Falls. He took it nice and slow, staying a few miles under the speed limit. No point in getting back to the station any sooner than necessary. Stone would probably just give him some other crappy job.

He turned on the radio, dialed in to the classic rock

station out of Plattsburgh, and tapped his fingers on the steering wheel to the beat of "Pour Some Sugar on Me" by Def Leppard. A few moments later he was singing along with the tune, belting out the lyrics in an awkward warble that would have won cringe-worthy karaoke night.

"I like it hot, sticky and sweet, from my head to my—"

A black SUV whipped out from a dirt road that accessed the power lines and slammed to a halt directly in front of him, blocking both lanes. Valentine stopped singing and started cursing as he stomped on his brakes to keep from broadsiding the vehicle.

"Damn it," he growled. "Somebody's going to jail for this stupidity."

He shifted the squad car into park, flipped on his red-and-blue emergency lights, and squelched off two short bursts from the siren to let the SUV know they were in trouble for their idiotic maneuver.

The SUV just sat there, idling. The windows were fully tinted so Valentine couldn't see inside. He knew he should probably be concerned but he was too jacked up on adrenaline and anger. He didn't feel like being cautious; he felt like dragging the driver out of the vehicle and teaching him a lesson.

He popped open his door, climbed out of his cruiser, and marched toward the SUV with purposeful, authoritative strides. "Hey!" he called out. "What the hell was that, you moron? You trying to get somebody killed?"

The driver's door of the SUV swung open, and a tall man dressed in black uncoiled from inside the cab. A black balaclava concealed his face.

"Shit!" Valentine immediately started to backpedal. He immediately regretted his rash recklessness. His hand dropped to the butt of his Glock as he tried to retreat to the cover of his car.

The man in black moved fast, bringing up his arm, some kind of ugly semi-automatic pistol in his fist. No suppressor, but no need – they were out in the middle of nowhere.

Valentine clawed at his holster, trying to get his gun free.

Too slow. Too late.

The man in black fired four times in rapid succession.

Valentine felt the hammering impacts as the bullets struck him, one going wide to shatter the windshield of his cruiser. He stumbled backward and suddenly found it difficult to stay on his feet. He went down hard but managed to draw his Glock before he hit the ground. Pain tore through his system. He heard someone screaming and recognized the sound of his own voice.

He got off a single shot as the man in black climbed back into the SUV, but saw it spark off the side-view mirror.

Then he saw nothing as the darkness engulfed him.

Stone drove over to the church and headed for the office. He nudged up the thermostat, sat down in his chair, and called Bester.

She answered on the first ring. "Bester."

"It's Stone."

"My favorite padre." The FBI agent sounded truly happy to hear from him. "How are things in Whisper Falls?"

"Homer Pressfield got ambushed. Bunch of bastards kicked the crap out of him. He's in the hospital."

"My God…"

"He told me he'd been receiving threatening notes from The Remnant."

Bester didn't immediately respond and during the silence, Stone's phone beeped. He glanced at the screen. An incoming call. He let it go to voicemail.

When Bester spoke, she sounded puzzled. "That's not their usual style. Cheap theatrics and telegraphed moves aren't how they play. They generally prefer to avoid publicity. And why Pressfield?"

Stone's phone beeped again. Another incoming call. He swiped it to voicemail.

"It's not like the guy is law enforcement or anything," Bester continued.

"He's been giving presentations at churches, talking about the intersection of religious and racial extremism. Maybe he was throwing too much light on their methodology, and they decided to send a message."

"We've been getting bits and pieces of information that definitely make it seem like they're planning something," Bester said. "We even found a connection between The Remnant and Cardine Trucking. Remember that asshole Rohmer? He's into occult shit."

Another beep. Another call. Stone was starting to get irritated.

"Rohmer has set up some sort of temple outside of Milford," Bester said. "It's a common dodge used by extremist groups – disguising themselves as a church. They know most judges are reluctant to authorize search warrants for religious institutions. It's the same concept as terrorists in the Middle East hiding weapons and explosives inside mosques."

"I've got a guy in Milford right now, digging into—" Stone stopped mid-sentence as he heard voices outside.

Apparently, Bester could hear them, too. "What's going on?"

"Not sure. I'll call you back." Stone hung up and headed

for the front door. He pulled it open just as Deputy Drummond was raising a fist to knock. His squad car was parked crookedly behind him, indicating he'd been in a rush.

Stone instantly knew something was wrong. "What happened?"

"Been trying to call you, sheriff."

"I know. Just tell me."

"It's Valentine." The senior deputy looked stricken. "He's been shot."

The rest of the day passed in a blur for Stone: the short drive to the station, the briefing, the update on Valentine's condition. The red-haired rookie had taken three rounds in the chest and stomach and been rushed to Plattsburgh for emergency surgery. His survival odds were fifty-fifty at best, Stone had been told.

The State troopers had coordinated with Milford PD to set up roadblocks to check every vehicle leaving town, but everyone knew it was a lost cause. Milford wasn't that big and whoever had gunned down Valentine was long gone before the police got any kind of dragnet in place.

The deputies – even the ones off-duty today – were prowling around the station like caged animals, worried about their fallen comrade and burning for payback when Drummond stuck his head into Stone's office.

"We've got Cade's dash cam, sheriff. You should be able to bring it up on your computer."

With Drummond watching over his shoulder, Stone logged into his workstation and clicked his way through a series of buttons that accessed the dash cam footage. On the monitor, the image of Route 3 appeared through the windshield of Valentine's cruiser as he drove back to Whisper Falls.

Stone watched as a black SUV barreled into view from the left-hand side and blocked the road. He immediately recalled what Pressfield had told him.

This black SUV just swerved right out in front of me…

Could this be the same vehicle? Stone didn't much believe in coincidences.

He stared at the screen grimly as Valentine exited the squad car, marched toward the SUV… and encountered a masked, black-clad gunman.

Drummond cursed as the gunner opened fire and Valentine went down. The dash cam footage became distorted by a bullet striking the windshield and splintering the glass.

Seconds later the SUV sped away. Through the jagged cracks in the windshield, Stone watched his deputy get off one shot, then just lay motionless in a spreading pool of blood.

Stone had watched men under his command fall before and it never got any easier.

Behind him, Drummond hissed, "I'm gonna kill that bastard."

As he watched the SUV disappear down the road, Stone thought, *Not if I get my hands on him first.*

TWENTY-SIX

EACH MORNING, Lucius Blake took up his sword and journeyed to the pagoda temple at the center of the Institute's sizable wooded property.

As always on brisk, cold mornings like this one, there was a stillness in the air. No traffic, no hubbub of voices or electronics. Birds clung to frozen tree branches, silent and motionless. Blake relished the quiet of these early hours. It gave him time to think and plan.

Blake opened the shoji sliding door that served as the entrance into the pagoda, the rice paper panels laminated to provide protection from the rain and snow.

He ducked beneath the lintel, careful not to bump his clean-shaven head. Inside was a large, wood-floored space, void of all trappings save one. Only a small wooden altar against the far wall gave any indication that the space held symbolic significance.

Blake kicked off his boots and sank into a kneeling position, his katana sheathed on the floor in front of him.

The techniques of *iaijutsu*, the art of drawing the Japanese katana sword, were many and exacting. Blake had studied each one thoroughly under a traditional master in Japan. He had practiced the forms faithfully every day since the age of twenty-one. Now nearing fifty-five, he found it ironic that his body had begun to deteriorate at exactly the moment when his mastery of the forms was peaking.

But that was the progression of life. For this reason, among many others, Blake believed that a man must pay attention to his legacy where his family, his business, and his community are concerned.

Above all else, where his race is concerned.

Meditation completed, Blake took up the sheathed katana, slid it beneath the wide cloth belt he wore, and paused to bring his breathing under absolute control.

Then his hands twitched and the blade flashed from the scabbard, its edge gleaming in the light of dawn. Still kneeling, Blake brought the blade down in *kiritsuke*—the finishing cut, the blow used to decapitate an enemy. Blake completed the technique and sheathed the sword.

He was displeased with his execution. By his reckoning, the technique would have been no more than seventy percent effective.

Blake hated weakness, despised it in himself as well as others. The cure for weakness? Discipline. And discipline with a purpose was the best discipline of all.

He readied himself to try again but was interrupted by a knock on the lintel. "Come," he called out.

The shoji door slid open to reveal Rich Rose, his second-in-command. "Sorry to disturb you, Colonel. Can I have a word with you?"

Blake relaxed his grip on the katana and sighed. He was not really a colonel, but organizations like The Remnant required a stable hierarchy to function properly and at peak performance levels, so he had appropriated the authoritarian title.

"What is it, Major?"

Rose wasn't really a major; that was just another of The Remnant's faux designations. In actuality, he was a slight, mousy man with glasses and a pencil-thin mustache who had a tendency to clear his throat frequently, some kind of nervous tic. Dressed in military fatigues, he resembled an accountant attending a Halloween costume party. "Sir, we have an update on our pipeline problem."

Still on his knees, Blake used his fists to swivel toward Rose. "Go on."

"One of our couriers was killed. Another has been picked up by the police. And one of the truckers, a man named Dorey, has been arrested for murder. Supposedly he ran over one of the bikers. Put it all together and it's slowed things down a bit."

Blake absorbed the news in silence.

"Dorey has obtained legal representation. The trial is scheduled for tomorrow, but it looks like the police are still investigating the matter."

"What makes you say that?"

"One of our scouts saw a Garrison County sheriff's deputy checking out the Cardine Trucking facility."

"And what did we do about that?"

"The deputy has been neutralized."

"Good." Blake stood up and put on his boots. "Maybe they'll think twice about digging deeper."

"Shooting a cop could mean trouble for us." Rose held open the shoji door for his boss.

"Trouble?" Blake shrugged. "That's what we live for, why we train. When you get right down to it, trouble is the entire purpose of our movement."

"Still," Rose persisted, "whacking a cop could bring some heat down on us. The kind of heat that slows things down."

Blake shook his head. "Not at this stage, major." They

walked outside and headed toward a large Quonset-style hut set back in the trees north of the temple. "Our plans are too far along to be stopped now. The pipeline's been interrupted? So what? It will take them time to figure out what's going on and we'll use that time to our advantage."

Blake and Rose entered the Quonset hut by a side door which opened directly into a private office. The room was tastefully appointed with carpeting, mahogany shelving, and works of art that alternated between Oriental and occultic in nature.

Blake removed the katana from his belt and leaned it against the desk as he took a seat behind it. "The last shipment from Cardine," he said. "It's been moved some-where secure?"

Rose nodded. "It's been put somewhere they'll never think to look."

"Good." Blake sighed. "Those trucks are the first of three priorities. The second priority is pushing those cops in Whisper Falls back a step. Put some fear in their hearts and let them know that nobody – *nobody* – fucks with The Remnant."

"And the third priority?"

"The goddamned bikers. We're going to exterminate them." Blake brought his fist down hard on the desk. "I want to see those Harleys turned into twisted, smoking wrecks. If I had my way, we'd crucify each and every one of the Children on the telephone poles between here and Whisper Falls."

Rose looked uncertain. "I'm guessing that's not an order, just wishful thinking."

"The crucifixion part, yeah. But we really are going to wipe out those hog-riding sons of bitches."

"Understood."

"But first things first," Blake said. "Pass the word to

the men. I want them to stage up and get ready to move those trucks. Do it quietly, just a couple at a time. The Cardine markings have been removed?"

"Painted over, yes, sir."

"Good." Blake reached for the phone on his desk. "You can go."

Rose fired off a quick salute and left as Blake dialed a number. The call was answered on the second ring.

"Kincaid."

"It's Blake. Is this line secure?"

"Of course. I figured I would be hearing from you."

"You figured right, General." Unlike the fake military titles The Remnant used, Lyle Kincaid actually *was* a Major General in the US Army. He was also loyal to the cause.

"I've been briefed on the recent developments," Kincaid said.

"Any updates on your end?"

"Things are getting hot. My contact in CID tells me that the sheriff over in Garrison County has been asking questions."

Blake clenched his teeth. Time to put this sheriff in a cheap pine box and send him to God under six feet of dirt.

"CID also got a visit from the FBI," General Kincaid said, sounding pissed. "And if the feds are involved, it means they've connected our efforts to those of our brothers-in-arms out of state." He paused, then added, "If they put it all together, we could be looking at conspiracy charges and a whole lot of time in a federal prison."

"So." Blake nodded, even though the general couldn't see him. "The enemy rears its head."

"Looks like it," Kincaid agreed. "Things are getting hot on my end. We have to shut the pipeline down."

"This is a good time to take a break," said Blake.

"We're pretty well stocked with what we need. My guys are trained and ready for action. They've just been waiting for a target and now they've got one. Or rather, more than one."

"The Children?"

"Those gutless grease suckers? I really couldn't care less about them but Rohmer's had a hard-on for the hog-riders ever since biker boy Roy turned his back on him, so we'll hunt them down. Part of the deal for Rohmer letting us use the Cardine trucks. But we need a bigger show of force than just wiping out some stupid bikers. We need to let Uncle Sam know who he's fucking with."

"What's your plan?"

Blake said, "We can't take on the FBI. Not yet. But a Podunk sheriff's department in a backwoods county? We'll leave them a smoking crater with no clues but the ones we want them to have."

Kincaid paused, considering. "It feels like it's too soon for direct action, but unfortunately, the fight has come to us."

"We have to send a message," Blake said firmly.

"Agreed. I'll leave that up to you." Kincaid hung up.

Blake dropped the phone back into its cradle, then stood up, stretched, and stepped out of his office into the spacious interior of the Quonset hut.

A row of gleaming black SUVs stretched to the rear doors. Warehouse shelving held a smorgasbord of boxes, crates, and containers. The bottom shelving was packed with gun racks bristling with row upon row of assault rifles. The upper shelves contained ammunition, grenades, and JC2 rocket launchers. The military pipeline had proven lucrative to the cause and a couple of dead soldiers was an easy price to pay, unfortunate sacrifices to a greater creed.

Blake let his fingers trace over a rifle barrel, equipped

with a flash suppressor, as he admired the collection of stolen Army hardware.

Over the past few years, under his guidance, The Remnant had successfully radicalized and recruited a small but growing number of US military personnel, and he had plans to expand into Canada as well. With Major General Kincaid organizing things on the Army base, the recruits – in coordination with their loyal partners in Cardine Trucking – had managed to smuggle all of the equipment now stacked on the shelves in front of him.

As the saying went, it was enough to equip a small army, and that's exactly what The Remnant was.

Blake knew that the country was politically polarized. Blacks and anarchists, doing the bidding of their Jew masters, were rioting, looting, and burning cities to the ground. A rising tide of white nationalism had altered public perception to the point where Blake and his acolytes weren't such a fringe group anymore. Increasing numbers of Americans were seeing though the manipulative, false flag, race-baiting lies of mainstream media and the socially-paralyzed weakness of the federal government.

Blake believed these Americas would rise up when the time came. The true patriots would stand up, dust off their boots, and unite against the rot and corruption and decay spreading through the country like a cancer. The kind of cancer that had no cure, so it had to be cut out and cauterized.

Because sometimes in order to bring something back to life, you first have to make it bleed.

It's time to bring the fight to the enemy, thought Blake.

Nothing could stop them now.

TWENTY-SEVEN

MASON HAD MORE briefcases than usual when Stone met him at the courthouse the next day. Apparently, the Dorey trial required a lot of paperwork.

"Need a hand?" Stone asked. It looked like Mason had more briefcases than fingers.

"Nah, I'm fine." Mason set his burden down on a nearby bench. "How's your deputy?"

"He made it through surgery but he's not out of the woods yet." Stone kept his voice level, not letting his tone betray the fact that he felt he should be out there hunting down Valentine's would-be murderer instead of sitting in a courtroom listening to legal mumbo-jumbo get tossed back and forth.

"Glad to hear it. As long as he's alive, there's still hope he'll pull through." Mason opened a briefcase and took out a file. "Today should be mostly procedural. The judge will have some questions since Slidell has done everything he can to throw up roadblocks and delays."

"Do we have a problem?"

"We'll find out." Mason glanced at his watch. "Courtroom Two. Let's get in there and see what happens."

Stone followed Mason into the courtroom. It wasn't large by any means, but bigger than you would expect for a small-town courthouse.

A handful of people occupied the visitors' gallery. Probably Dorey's family, if Stone had to guess. Dorey himself sat at the defense table next to Slidell.

"Ah!" Slidell's oily smile flashed as they approached. "So nice to see you, counselor."

"Morning, Scott," Mason grumbled, ignoring Slidell's outstretched hand as he slumped into his seat.

"And Sheriff Stone." Slidell bowed mockingly. "So good of you to be here."

Stone figured telling the lawyer what he thought of him probably wasn't the best way to kick off the trial, so he kept his mouth shut as he sat down next to Mason.

He turned his head as a trio of men entered the room and settled themselves in the gallery. Stone immediately sensed there was something off about them.

"Looks like we've got an audience," he said.

The prosecutor shrugged. "The trial is open to the public." He wrangled files on the table in front of him. Open briefcases ringed his chair. "A day in court can be just as entertaining as the movies. Even better, it's free."

"Great," Stone muttered. "Maybe tomorrow I'll bring some popcorn."

"Not sure Jaramillo would appreciate that."

Stone turned his head enough to see the courtroom behind him. He wasn't subtle about who he was looking at, nor did he care. His eyes settled on the trio that had triggered his internal alarm system and set him on edge. They were all dressed in black, sitting with arms crossed and staring right back at him as if trying to convey some kind of unspoken threat. He didn't recognize any of them.

He tried to shrug off the uneasy feeling as the bailiff

called the room to order and introduced the judge. Stone faced front again as Judge Jaramillo took her seat and looked at Mason.

"Counselor, are you ready to proceed?"

Mason stood up. "Yes, I am, your honor. As your honor is no doubt aware, the Garrison County Sheriff's Department recently suffered a tragic setback in the ongoing investigation. Deputy Cade Valentine was ambushed and shot multiple times following an investigation of the Cardine Trucking facility. He—"

"Objection, your honor." Slidell sounded disgusted as he rose to his feet. "While we are all truly sorry for Deputy Valentine's misfortune, let's not gild the lily. He was shot during a routine traffic stop. There is no evidence it had anything to do with this case."

Stone heard the courtroom door open and turned his head again as another trio of men, all dressed in black, entered the courtroom. They sat down in the visitor's gallery and stared hard at him, eyes flinty and hostile.

Stone felt like there was a big ol' bullseye emblazoned on his back. These boys were bad news, no doubt about it.

Meanwhile, Slidell was busy tap dancing all over Mason's case.

"...in addition, your honor, there are aspects of the discovery portion of this case that are troubling. On defense Exhibit Three, for example, you will note that there was a break in the chain of evidence..."

Now it was Mason's turn to object. "Your honor, defense counsel is playing administrative games, hoping to derail this case on a technicality because he knows he can't do it on the merits. There is no break. I have personally reviewed the chain of evidence for each exhibit and it's—"

"Your honor," Slidell interrupted, holding up a notecard. "I have here the evidence tag for Exhibit Three. Please note the blank space between the third and fourth signatures."

Damn, Stone thought. Was this really how this case was going to play out? Listening to Slidell throw legalese bullshit around further eroded his faith in the system he was sworn to uphold.

He still believed that justice could be found in a court-room. But sometimes the law failed, and when that happened, a more primal justice, one not protected by the honor of the badge, was called for.

As Mason argued his defense of the evidence, Stone heard yet another person enter the courtroom. He turned his head again and saw another man dressed in black take a seat at the very front of the visitor's gallery.

The newcomer was a burly man with massive shoulders and a shaved head. He looked at Stone the way a hunter might line up his gunsights to squeeze off a shot. Stone felt cold apprehension sweep through him. He was being watched and he didn't like it. Not one damn bit.

All seven of the men in black stared at him – pointedly, fixedly, menacingly. They wanted him to feel their hostility.

Stone did his best to ignore them as the legal battle rolled on and Slidell pulled out all the stops. After an hour, Judge Jaramillo called a recess without proceedings having even reached opening arguments.

"Slidell is turning this into a damn paper chase," Mason fumed as they left the courtroom. "We'll be dealing with procedural crap for at least the next two hours."

"Is there going to be a problem?" Stone asked.

"Don't worry, I'll do my best to make sure our case doesn't go down the toilet."

Stone scanned the courthouse lobby. No sign of the men in black.

"I've got to swing by the office." Mason consulted the clock on the wall. "Really no reason for you to hang around. I'll give you a call when we start getting into the meat and potatoes of the trial."

"Sounds good." Stone parted company with Mason and headed out across the parking lot toward his Blazer. A piece of paper had been tucked under one of the windshield wipers. He tugged it loose and unfolded it.

There, emblazoned in red, was a crucifix with swastikas adorning the tip and ends of both arms. The profane cross was set within an inverted pentagram inside a trapezoid. A cold chill that had nothing to do with the weather passed through him as he recalled Homer Pressfield's words:

"The Remnant calls this The Sickle. They believe it projects actual occult power."

Stone gritted his teeth, feeling a deep fury starting to boil up inside him.

The wolves were closing in.

But they had mistaken a predator for prey.

———

Stone drove to his house and made sure all the doors were locked before he went down into the basement, Max trailing behind him like a silent, loyal shadow.

At the bottom of the stairs, he hit the switch to turn on the lights, then pivoted toward the large, biometric gun safe recessed into the wall. He pressed his thumb to the scanner, heard a mechanical click deep inside the vault, and the door popped open.

A rack of rifles gleamed in the fluorescent glow of the basement lighting. Stone picked up the Heckler & Koch

UMP-45. The blowback closed-bolt rifle, capable of firing upwards of 600 rounds of .45 ACP ammunition per minute, was popular with spec-ops warriors and Stone was no exception. Like the HK-416 carbine beside it, the UMP-45 was not available for civilian purchase, but Stone possessed a Class 3 federal firearms license that permitted him to own full-auto weapons.

Stone double-checked both guns, making sure they were in working order. He then turned his attention to his preferred hunting rifle, a Seekins Precision Havak Pro. With its 26-inch beveled barrel, carbon composite frame and threaded muzzle, the Havak was the Cadillac of hunting rifles. Capable of putting a .338 Win Mag round downrange at over 500 yards with perfect accuracy, the Havak was a smart choice for precision long-range shooting. Stone had topped it with a Bushnell Elite Tactical 6 scope, a high-grade optic if ever there was one.

On an upper shelf was an array of handguns. His massive Smith & Wesson Stealth Hunter Performance .44 Magnum revolver dominated, but there were some semi-autos there too. His warrior days had made him adept with semi-auto pistols, but Stone was a wheel gun man at heart. He just appreciated the clean, non-jamming simplicity of a six-shooter.

Stacked behind the handguns were boxes of ammunition and on the shelf below, a dozen M67 fragmentation grenades, looking like dull green eggs nobody had found at Easter.

Stone considered The Sickle stuck on his windshield to be a declaration of war. The black-clad men in the courtroom had been there to send a message:

You're being hunted, sheriff.

He had his duty-carry Glock .45 on his right hip, his Colt Cobra .38 snub-nosed in his right coat pocket for backup, and a Benchmade Bedlam 860 tactical folding knife clipped into the left pocket of his jeans. He tucked one of the grenades into his left coat pocket for good measure; it balanced out the weight of the Colt. He had no idea where or when The Remnant would strike, and it never hurt to have an explosive option on hand.

Stone closed the gun safe and pressed the button that slid the mechanical locking mechanisms back in place.

He looked at Max grimly. "If they want a war, I'll give 'em one."

TWENTY-EIGHT

STONE DECIDED it had been too long since he'd seen Holly, so he drove down to the Birch Bark to grab a cup of coffee. With The Remnant cranking up the heat, Stone didn't know when he would get another chance to spend time with her.

There was also the chance that he wouldn't be the last man standing when this war was over. He wasn't so naïve as to believe that he was too good to catch a bullet. Many warriors didn't live to be old men and he didn't want to meet his Maker without seeing Holly again. He just prayed it wasn't the last time.

"Howdy, stranger." Holly smiled and poured Stone a cup of coffee as he entered the diner. As if reading his mind, she put it in a to-go cup.

It was the back end of a busy lunch hour and a half dozen tables were still occupied. Stone recognized that she wouldn't have much time for him right now. Fair enough. He'd been busy, she was busy. That was life sometimes.

He leaned against the counter. "Thanks," he said, accepting the coffee, not displeased when their fingertips brushed together. "Sorry I haven't been around much. Things have been busy."

"I heard the trial isn't going well."

"It's a shit show."

"You'll have to tell me all about it." She looked at him regretfully. "But it'll have to be another time." She moved off to take care of her customers, flashing him a quick goodbye smile.

Stone left some money on the counter to pay for his coffee. When he turned to leave, he nearly bumped into Sonny, the biker stepdad of Lizzy's friends.

"Hey, sheriff." Sonny didn't look happy. "Got a sec?"

"Sure. Something wrong?"

"Need to talk to you."

"Want to grab a table?"

The biker glanced left and right, clearly uncomfortable being seen fraternizing with the law. "No. Outside."

They exited the diner and Stone followed Sonny around the side of the building, where the biker lit a smoke.

"There's been some shit going down," Sonny said without preamble. "The Children have had a couple of incidents on the road the last couple of days."

"What do you mean by 'incidents'?"

"Somebody's bird-dogging us," Sonny growled. "Two of the brothers reported being followed while they rode. Said it was like the driver was *trying* to be noticed. Like they were trying to send a message or something."

"Was it the same person both times?"

Sonny shrugged. "Hard to tell with tinted windows. But it was definitely the same vehicle both times. Black SUV."

Stone thought of the bastard in the black SUV ambushing and gunning down Valentine. Anger stirred within him.

"They tried to take Daryl out last night," Sonny said. "Followed him for a few miles, then raced up next to him and tried to sideswipe him off the road."

"Looks like these sons of bitches are out for blood."

"Well, they didn't get it last night. Daryl managed to dodge the sideswipe and pulled out his gun and the SUV took off like his ass was on fire. But something tells me they're gonna keep on coming. Thought you might want to know."

"I appreciate the information."

Without another word, Sonny tossed his cigarette into a snowbank, turned around, and walked away. Stone watched him go, the pieces starting to click together in his mind.

———

Stone needed some time to think things through and pull the pieces together in his head. He saddled up Rocky and rode down the logging trail that led into the large field on the back edge of his property, nestled up against state land.

It looked like The Remnant was behind everything. The dead Yankee Doodle Dandies, the attack on Pressfield, the attempted murder of Deputy Valentine, the courtroom intimidation. He wasn't clear on the connection between The Remnant and Cardine Trucking yet, but judging from Sonny's information, it looked like The Remnant had joined the trucker's war against the bikers.

In other words, there was a whole lot of bad shit going on in his county, all coming from a single source. There were wicked people out there running around and they needed prison or a bullet and Stone didn't much care which. He just wanted the criminal cancer cleaned out of his town.

Easier said than done.

Then again, Stone was perfectly willing to take the hard road.

The Remnant was a shadow force. Most white supremacist groups were happy to step into the limelight and share their vile beliefs, but the more dangerous ones lurked below the radar. The Remnant was such a group, perhaps more lethal than all the others, given their recruitment of active military members and their willingness to engage in violent bloodshed. Their creed might be psychotic bullshit, but the carnage created in its name was not.

Stone had served his country as a warrior, the kind of man called upon to do grim things in dark places in the name of freedom and justice. During that time, he had interacted with every branch of the US military, from the grunts humping it across desert wastelands to the four-star generals in the Pentagon's air-conditioned offices. And while there had been a few bad apples along the way, the overwhelming majority demonstrated absolute loyalty to their oath. They served with conviction because they believed they served a just cause.

So how did The Remnant manage to lure so many good soldiers to betray that oath and become traitors to their country?

Stone steered Rocky off his property onto a narrow riding trail that threaded through the thick woods on state land. It ran 500 yards or so before emerging onto a rarely used gravel road that ran alongside a narrow brook with marshy wetlands on either side. These kinds of back roads could be found all through the sparsely populated portions of Garrison County, used primarily by hunters looking for an unpopulated place to sight in their rifles or teenagers looking for privacy to park and party.

Stone gently nudged Rocky's sides, directing the horse out onto the road, his mood still contemplative. Evil had come to his quiet little town and he didn't like it, not one damn bit. One way or another, The Remnant needed to be eradicated.

Stone heard the sound of an approaching vehicle, gravel crunching under the tires, but didn't think anything of it. The road didn't get used much, but it did get used. He guided Rocky over to the side so the vehicle could pass.

Seconds later, he learned that passing them wasn't what the driver had in mind.

The black SUV barreled around the corner and gunned the gas, engine screaming, and bore down on them like a heat-seeking missile locked on target.

Stone jerked Rocky to the side and threw himself out of the saddle. He prayed the horse managed to get out of the way in time. He felt one of his boots catch in the stirrup for a heart-freezing half-second, then he was sailing through the air.

He landed hard on the frozen marshland as the SUV howled through the space he and Rocky had just occupied. He breathed a sigh of relief to see the Appaloosa still standing. The stallion reared up on its hind legs and pawed at the air, looking both frightened and angry.

Stone powered up into a kneeling position, the Colt Cobra in his fist. The SUV skidded around in a tight turn and came back for another pass. Stone dumped two bullets into the grill, hoping to rip open the radiator, but no luck.

The big SUV couldn't come too far out into the marsh, so Stone retreated further back onto the ice, hoping it would hold his weight and not send him breaking through into frigid water. The vehicle swept past him again, the driver anonymous behind tinted windows but dead set on ending Stone's life.

The SUV spun through another turn and just sat in the middle of the road 50 yards away, engine rumbling like the hungry growl of a large predator.

Stone rose to his feet and glared at the windshield. All he could see was the reflection of the trees. But that didn't stop him from sending his angry gaze through the glass at the person behind the wheel. Letting the driver know they had fucked with the wrong preacher.

Stone knew better than most that sometimes violence is the only answer, the only language that bad men understand. And he spoke it fluently.

He also knew that sometimes offense is the best defense.

Face grim, revolver in his right hand, Stone left the ice and ran toward the SUV.

He could almost sense the driver's hesitation. Hunters are always surprised when the prey attacks. Stone closed the distance in seconds.

The SUV's engine revved into a scream and the vehicle surged forward. Stone dodged inside the turning radius of the front wheels. His gun barked twice, puncturing the front and rear tires on the driver's side.

The vehicle skidded to a halt, the rear fishtailing toward Rocky, who nimbly dodged clear. The horse snorted aggressively and trotted off into the cover of the woods.

Stone leveled the Colt at the crippled SUV. *Time for you to die, you son of a bitch.*

He fired into the driver's side window. The round ricocheted off, spalling the glass. He sent his next shot into the door panel, denting but not penetrating. Clearly the SUV sported armored body panels and bullet-resistant glass.

But what about the undercarriage?

Time to find out.

Stone pulled the grenade from his pocket, jerked out the pin, and tossed it under the SUV. The results were lethal.

The blast sounded like demons shrieking in hell. The air shuddered and throbbed against Stone's eardrums as the vehicle blossomed in a curtain of fire. Shrapnel shredded open the fuel tank and a secondary explosion rocked the vehicle, flames shooting skyward in orange tendrils.

The detonation turned the SUV into a twisted, burning wreck. Stone caught a glimpse inside the engulfed cab, the driver melting behind the wheel like a scarecrow caught in an inferno.

Stone stood there and watched it all burn. He would leave it here for The Remnant to find. A trophy at the edge of his property, marking his kill, sending a message back to them.

He wasn't interested in arresting any of them. Like their charbroiled comrade in the SUV, they needed to face a brand of justice that was far more primal and scorching hot. They needed to feel the heat.

Stone stared into the flames, jaw clenched. Looked like hell had come to Whisper Falls.

TWENTY-NINE

STONE NEEDED ANSWERS. And he knew just where to start.

Slidell, for all his sleazebag lawyer tactics, had still not managed to spring his client from custody. Dorey remained behind bars at the station.

After putting Rocky back in the barn, Stone jumped in the Blazer and headed toward town, calling ahead to have Dorey moved to an interview room. In front of him, the sinking sun sent golden fire blazing across the faces of the mountains while the canyons and crevices sank deeper into blackening shadows. Off in the distance behind him, the SUV burned down to a charred husk with a smoldering skeleton inside, his message to The Remnant. The thought caused a cold smile to tighten his face.

Dusk had fallen by the time Stone reached town. Main Street wasn't very busy as he drove past businesses closing up shop for the day. He pulled into the sheriff's station parking lot and headed inside.

"Evening, sheriff." The young deputy, Sanchez, stood as Stone entered. She was the newest addition to the force, a rookie so wet behind the ears, she made Valentine look like a seasoned veteran. Still, she had done remarkably well at the training academy.

"Evening, deputy." He motioned for her to sit back down. "Any word on Valentine?"

"He's stable, sir. I checked in with the hospital about thirty minutes ago."

"Glad to hear it. You move Dorey like I asked?"

"Interview Room Two. Want me to get you a coffee?"

"Sure, that'd be great."

Stone went into the darkened observation cubicle with the one-way glass that looked into the interview room. Dorey was handcuffed to the table, dressed in jailhouse orange that managed to seem drab despite the bright color.

Sanchez entered moments later and handed him a cup of coffee. "Will you need a witness, sir?"

"No witnesses." Stone took a quick sip of the coffee and then dumped the rest all over the recording equipment. "In fact, I think now would be a good time for you to clean the video camera."

Sanchez looked surprised for a moment but recovered quickly, a savvy grin spreading across her face. "That's quite a spill, sir. I'll get on it right away." She switched off the recording console and went back to her desk.

Stone knew his actions wouldn't hold much weight in court – he could almost feel Judge Jaramillo's disapproving scowl already – but it was better than nothing.

He took a deep breath and exhaled it, long and slow.

Time to play.

Stone walked into the interrogation room, closed the door behind him, and leaned against the wall.

"Let me get right to the point," he said to Dorey. "This conversation is off the record. We never talked, got it?"

Dorey looked wary and confused. "What are you trying to say?"

Stone crossed his arms. "I'm saying this isn't being recorded."

"Why not?"

"Because I'm going to tell you some things I shouldn't. But things that I think you should know."

Dorey's eyes widened. "Like what?" he asked.

Stone knew he had the trucker on the hook. "We've grabbed up a couple members of The Remnant. We also managed to hunt down your buddy Rohmer. Took the squealing little bitch about all of two seconds to roll over on you and the other truckers."

"You're lying."

"I'm not lying," Stone lied. "He threw you all under the bus. Got himself some fancy law firm out of Albany to handle his defense. Even figured out a way to beat the conspiracy rap."

"What's that mean, exactly?" Dorey asked.

"He admits there was a conspiracy. He just says he had nothing to do with it, that it was all your idea."

Stone let Dorey stew on that for a solid minute, letting the misinformation act like a slow corrosive, eating away at his confidence.

Finally, the trucker said, "So what do you have in mind?"

"Straight-forward plea deal. I can get you released tonight, all charges dropped, if you give me actionable intel on The Remnant."

"The Remnant?" Dorey nodded. "I'll tell you anything you want to know."

"Where are they?"

"You know the woods west of Milford? Between the

city and the county line? There's a place back there. Sign out front calls it the Hermetic Institute."

The door opened abruptly and Sanchez stuck her head in. "Sheriff, you need to see this right now." Panic simmered in her voice.

Dorey caught it too. "What's going on?"

Stone said, "Stay here."

The trucker angrily rattled the handcuffs securing him to the table. "Where the fuck else would I go?"

Stone didn't bother responding as he followed Sanchez out of the room. "What the hell's going on, deputy?"

"Look!" She pointed out the front window.

Three black SUVs hunkered in the park across the street. As he watched, they switched on their high beams in a synchronized sequence, one after another, blasting the building with light.

"I think we've got some trouble," Sanchez said.

"Yeah, I don't think they're here to sell us Girl Scout cookies," Stone replied.

If they were about to fight off an attack from heavily armed neo-Nazis, they needed to upgrade their weaponry. Stone led Sanchez into his office where he kept a rack of AR-15 rifles. They rarely had use for this level of long-range, high-capacity firepower in Garrison County, but Stone made sure the tactical rifles stayed cleaned and oiled just in case.

He tossed one to Sanchez. "Lock and load."

"Shit about to hit the fan, sir?"

"Not sure, but we'll be ready if it does."

"Copy that."

Stone slapped in a magazine, shoved two more into his coat pockets, and then went back out front.

The SUVs had not moved. They looked like hungry

beasts, ready to pounce. Stone reached over and killed the lights. No point in making themselves easy targets.

"Who are they?" Sanchez asked.

"Neo-Nazis."

"Really? White supremacists?"

Stone nodded.

Sanchez racked the charging handle on her rifle, putting a round in place. "Then I guess I won't feel bad about shooting any of them."

The door of the center SUV opened, and a man emerged holding a bullhorn. He stepped out in front of the vehicles, silhouetted in the glare of the bristling high beams. As he raised the bullhorn and flicked it on, a shimmer of feedback floated across the park.

"Stone!" the electronically amplified voice called out. "We know you're in there."

Sanchez shifted. Stone glanced over and saw she was head down in her gunsights, thumb hovering over the assault rifle's safety selector switch.

"Just give me the greenlight," she said, "and I'll start putting holes in these *pendejos*."

"Not yet."

"Stone!" The man with the bullhorn sounded impatient. "You've got one minute to release Roger Dorey or we're coming in, whether you like it or not."

Sanchez snapped her rifle to semi-auto.

Stone counted down the numbers in his head. He could feel the adrenaline surging through his system but the blood in his veins still felt cool. He was aware of the tension rising but refused to let fear shape his response.

Twenty seconds…twenty-one… twenty-two…

Stone spotted men emerging from the SUVs, shadow shapes ghosting behind the headlights' glare, gripping what appeared to be assault rifles. It was impossible to tell exactly how many there were, but clearly he and Sanchez were outnumbered.

Forty-three... forty-four... forty-five...

"Time's almost up," the man shouted into the bull-horn, accompanied by another shriek of feedback. "What's it going to be? Is Dorey coming out or are we coming in?"

Fifty-eight... fifty-nine...

The bullhorn-man looked over his shoulder at the men with the guns, pointed at the front of the sheriff's station, and bellowed, "Light 'em up, boys!"

Stone and Sanchez surged upright and triggered a hail of bullets at the SUVs outside as the last word was leaving the man's lips. They fired right through the front window, collapsing it in an avalanche of glittering shards. Unable to pinpoint the gunmen lurking beyond the blinding high beams, they aimed for the vehicles instead.

Sanchez's rounds ripped through the headlights and raked the hood of the SUV on the right. Stone rapid-fired a fusillade that shredded the tires of the one on the left as the man dropped the bullhorn and leaped back into the center vehicle.

Stone and Sanchez eased off their triggers as the two SUVs that still had rubbers on their rims backed off, whipping around to take cover behind the band shell about fifty yards away, at the north end of the park.

Cold air rushed in through the shattered window and carried with it the wailing of sirens in the distance. Prob-ably state troopers responding to the unexpected sound of gunfire ravaging the usually quiet town. They'd be here in mere minutes, Stone knew. He and Sanchez just had to survive until then.

"How you doing on ammo, Sanchez?"

"Just topped off with a new mag, sir."

"Good. You're gonna need it."

In the park across the street, short bursts of auto fire shattered the streetlamps and plunged the scene into darkness. Stone glimpsed men skulking through the shadows, brandishing weapons. Looked like they were planning one more assault attempt before they fled the scene. A last-ditch, now or never scenario as the pulsing red glow of fast-approaching police units suffused the night.

Two men peeled off from the others, crouched behind a concrete park bench, and readied their rifles. Stone recognized the maneuver they were trying to pull off: the two men would provide cover fire to keep Stone and Sanchez's heads down while the others moved to breach the front door.

Stone wasn't waiting around for that to happen.

"Give 'em hell," he growled.

Stone brought his AR-15 to bear and squeezed off a triple-burst. He saw one of the men behind the park bench punched backward as the top of his head came apart like a sledgehammered egg.

Sanchez opened fire as well, her steady, rhythmic shooting keeping the would-be breachers at bay. As they sought cover behind benches and statues, she drilled a pair of slugs into the back of a gunner's leg. He crumpled with a snarled cry of pain until her follow-up shot tore into his temple and shut him up forever.

The survivors returned fire as they retreated, muzzle flashes winking like oversized fireflies. The sirens were closing in. Backup would be here in less than a minute. Stone heard the attacker's shouted curses as they scrambled back to the SUVs.

"That's right," Sanchez muttered as she performed a tactical reload, swapping out her partially depleted magazine for a fresh one. "Get the hell out of here, you sorry-ass cockroaches."

The scream of the sirens rose in volume as the assault team piled into the two remaining SUVs and raced off into the night.

Stone turned to Sanchez. "Put Dorey back in his cell and stand watch. Anybody you don't know tries to get him out, give them two to the chest and one to the head."

"Copy that, sir."

Stone ran outside as a State Police cruiser skidded to a stop in front of the station. He slid into the passenger seat and pointed in the direction the attackers had fled. "Suspects took off that way. Two black SUVs going north on Main Street, probably heading for Route 3."

The trooper whipped around in a tire-smoking 180, keeping just one hand on the wheel while the other snatched up the radio mic. "All units, BOLO on two black SUVs, last seen northbound through Whisper Falls, possibly heading for Route 3."

"I gotcha, state!" Stone recognized Drummond's voice. "This is Drummond with the Garrison County Sheriff's Department. I'm coming in from the opposite direction so I'll see if I can cut them off."

"Ten-four, Drummond." The state trooper dropped the mic and slalomed off Main Street onto Route 3, tires screeching for traction on the cold asphalt.

Thirty seconds later they thumped over the old railroad tracks and the lights of town receded in the rear view mirror. They raced down the empty stretch of rural highway at over 90 mph. Stone prayed they didn't hit a patch of black ice that would either send them crashing into the rock ledges to their left or spinning into the river to their right. He wasn't afraid to die but that didn't mean he wanted to do it tonight.

The road snaked alongside the river until it finally straightened into a mile-long stretch by the school bus garage.

At the other end of the straightaway, Stone saw the flashing lights of Drummond's cruiser, closing the distance fast. There was no sign of the SUVs. Either they weren't on this stretch of road or they were running without headlights to avoid detection.

Stone checked his AR-15, then cracked the window. If the SUVs were running dark, they could be on them in seconds. He needed to be ready to fire at a moment's notice.

The radio swarmed with chatter.

"...about a mile behind you and closing fast!"

"...chopper will be in the air in five minutes."

"...coming down Trudeau Hill Road to make sure they didn't cut over to Route 86."

Drummond's flashers loomed ever closer through the darkness. Stone kept the AR-15 at the ready, scanning the night for any sign of the SUVs.

Moments later, Drummond's cruiser braked to a halt. The state trooper did the same, rolling to a stop just a few yards away.

"Dammit!" Stone growled. "Where the hell did they go?"

It was like the SUVs had vanished into thin air.

THIRTY

THE SEARCH DRAGGED on into the early hours of the morning, all parties too stubborn to admit they'd been bested. The State Police helicopter pilot earned his keep while ground units from local law enforcement patrolled the roads, looking for some sign of where the SUVs had gone. But nothing turned up. Stone eventually sent everyone home and went back to the station.

Sanchez was still there. She had cleaned up the debris from the firefight, hung a tarp over the broken window, and set up a portable electric heater to ward off the cold air seeping in. She was sitting at a computer terminal when Stone walked in and sank wearily into a chair across from her. He rubbed his bloodshot eyes. It had been a long damn night.

"Sir, why don't you go home and grab some shut-eye?" Sanchez said, sounding worried. "The day-shift deputies will be here in another couple hours to keep an eye on the shop. One thing I learned in the Marines is that a leader does more harm than good if they're exhausted."

Stone gave her a frank look. "How are you doing?"

"Fine, sir. A little tired but not too bad."

"That's not what I meant."

"Then what did you mean?"

"You killed a man tonight, Sanchez. Some people have a hard time living with that."

"I was a Marine, sir. Two tours in the sandbox. Tonight wasn't the first time I killed somebody."

"Fair enough." Stone stood up. "I'll get some rest after I finish with Dorey. Do me a favor, put him back in the interrogation room, then take the rest of the night off. You earned it."

"Copy that, sir."

When Stone joined Dorey in the interview room fifteen minutes later, he found the prisoner gazing blearily into a cup of coffee Sanchez had provided him, steam twisting off the surface of the java like little dancing ghosts. But he became animated when he saw Stone.

"What the hell happened? One minute I'm in here spilling my guts and then the next thing I know, it sounds like World War III out there and your deputy shows up with an assault rifle and hustles me back to my cage."

"The Remnant paid us a visit." Stone fixed his eyes on Dorey. "They came here for you. When we wouldn't hand you over, they shot up the place."

"Anybody dead?"

"Nobody that matters. Just two Remnant members." Stone stared at him grimly. "I think you better keep talking before I tell the mortician we need a third coffin."

"Yeah, yeah, sure. We still have a deal, right?"

"Nothing's changed. Keep talking. You were telling me about some institute."

"Yeah. The Hermetic Institute. In the woods between

Milford and the county line. Used to be some kind of summer camp but it closed back in 2015. The Remnant bought the property a couple years ago. Put up perimeter fencing. Rebuilt most of the buildings. I think it's listed on the official books as some sort of religious retreat. You know, to dodge the taxman and keep the cops from digging too deep."

"Who runs the place?"

"Guy named Lucius Blake. A real sick son of a bitch."

"What makes you say that?"

"Just things I've heard. Word is, Blake messes around with some satanic shit."

Stone remembered Sonny telling him Rohmer was connected to the occult scene, so this information tracked, and further cemented the connection between The Remnant and Cardine Trucking.

He asked, "How many people at the institute?"

"I've only been there once," Dorey replied. "There was a fair number back then. Maybe fifty? Seventy-five? Something like that. All pretty serious operators too. Ex-military guys. They have stockpiles of weapons, ammo, vehicles, explosives. Enough for something big, that's for sure."

"So what are they planning?"

"I'm not in the loop on that. You'd have to ask Lucius Blake."

"Don't worry, I plan on it."

Stone put Dorey back in his cell, the trucker yowling the whole time about his deal, then went back to his office. He put a quick call in to the hospital to check on Valentine – no change – and then leaned back in his chair, tempted to just sleep right there. His eyes felt heavier than two cement blocks.

Sanchez had not obeyed his instructions to go home. She sat at her computer, ignoring the annoying sound of the tarp flapping in the broken window, nudged by an insistent, cold wind trying to sneak past the seal and steal the warmth.

After fighting sleep for a few minutes, Stone got up, shoved on his Stetson, and shrugged into his coat. He would get a warrant once the sun came up and pay The Remnant a visit at the Hermetic Institute. Until then, it was time to go home, check on Max, and pass out for a few hours. It wouldn't be enough to fully revitalize him, but hopefully it would take the edge off his fatigue.

You're getting old, an inner voice told him. *Was a time when you could go without sleep for four days straight and still get the job done.*

Stone sighed. It was true, but that had been years ago, and those years felt like a distant, half-remembered lifetime. Back when the world – and his worldview – had been a simpler place. Back when he had never questioned whether his killing was righteous or wrong.

He shook off the introspection. Now was not the time for such thoughts. He said goodbye to Sanchez and stepped outside into the cold breeze. It was that strange time of night when the world seemed to hold its breath. To the east, the darkness turned a subtle shade lighter, preparing for the arrival of dawn in a few hours.

In the parking lot, Stone examined his Blazer, checking for any damage incurred during the firefight. Everything looked intact, something of a minor miracle. He had expected at least a flat tire or a few bullet holes. At least something had gone right tonight. He breathed a silent prayer of thanks.

Starting up the Blazer, he pulled out of the lot and

angled out of town, traffic nonexistent at this time of night. It was so quiet, he could practically hear the electronic buzz of the traffic lights as he passed beneath them.

As he neared the trailer park where Deputy Drummond lived, he spotted a pillar of smoke smudging the sky. Could be a trash burn – the wet winter months were ideal for incinerating stuff that might spark a wildfire during the dry heat of summer – but it was pretty early in the morning for that sort of thing.

Stone felt his heart start to beat a little faster. As he drove closer to the trailer park, the orange hue of a large blaze formed a corona over the pine trees. Too big to be an ordinary bonfire lit by some insomniac drunks looking to burn their garbage.

He rounded the bend and to his horror, saw Drummond's trailer engulfed in flames. He skidded to a stop at the park's entrance, activated his emergency lights, radioed for assistance, and went running over.

He found Drummond on his knees in the snow, cradling the limp form of his cat to his chest, weeping without shame. Stone put a comforting hand on the old deputy's shoulder.

"No," Drummond whispered. "Please, God, no...not Barney...not my best friend..."

The trailer was a roiling ball of flame. Drummond's neighbors gathered outside their own homes, silently expressing their sympathies and watching to ensure the conflagration didn't spread to the other homes. One guy held a garden hose in his hand. Against this inferno, that would be like fighting a dragon with a water pistol.

As Stone watched, the roof of Drummond's trailer collapsed. Sparks spiraled into the sky to get snuffed out by the winter wind. The tires melted, pooling into black lakes of sizzling rubber. Inside the blaze, glass jars and cans popped like firecrackers as the intense heat exploded their pressurized contents.

At the other end of town, Stone heard the first sirens pierce the night as the Whisper Falls Volunteer Fire Department rolled toward the scene.

He turned his attention back to Drummond, still clutching his dead cat, choking on sobs. He didn't know what to say, so he said nothing. Sometimes in the midst of a tragedy, the best thing you could do for someone was just be there.

When his phone rang, he took his hand off Drummond's shoulder and answered. "This is Stone."

"I know who you are." The voice on the other end sounded both calm and menacing. "Do you know who I am?"

"Really not in the mood for games right now," Stone rasped.

"My name is Lucius Blake, sheriff, and you look like a fool standing next to a washed-up old man holding a dead cat."

Stone didn't waste time scanning the darkness. This was a mountain region, with thick woods and tall cliffs all around offering a thousand places for concealment, especially in the dead of night. He wouldn't be able to spot Blake unless the man wanted to be spotted, which clearly wasn't the case.

"I think it's time we had ourselves a heart to heart," Blake said. "Let's call a temporary truce. After all, I put one of your deputies in the hospital and just burned another one out of his home after stomping the piss out of his beloved pet. You, in turn, killed two of my men tonight. I wouldn't say the scales are evenly balanced but let's call it close enough and have a chat, sheriff." Blake paused. "Bear in mind, Stone, this is a one-time offer. Turn me down and we go back to war mode, and I promise you the next bullet fired will take off the back of your deputy's head."

Stone ached to smash the bastard's teeth down his throat. In fact, he might just do that when they met, truce be damned.

He said, "I pick where, you pick when."

THIRTY-ONE

STONE MANAGED to get everything set up with remarkable speed.

First, he called Bester and started bringing her up to speed on everything that had happened. She didn't even let him finish.

"I'm on my way," she said and hung up.

Next, he secured a warrant to search the Hermetic Institute. That done, Stone contacted the local PDs to coordinate SWAT support for the raid.

His last call was to the State Police to arrange for their helicopter to hover just outside audible range during the meet between him and Blake, scheduled for less than an hour from now, and be prepared to tail The Remnant leader when he left. Despite the last minute call, the state boys were happy to help.

Stone left his gun belt draped over the back of his chair. He and Blake had agreed they would both be unarmed for the meet, though they were each allowed to have an armed bodyguard watching their back. Of course, Stone had no intention of abiding by the no-guns rule; he dropped the Colt Cobra .38 snub-nosed revolver into his coat pocket before heading out to the parking lot where Drummond waited beside the Blazer, looking madder than a bee-stung pit bull.

Stone studied his deputy. "Sure you're up for this?"

Drummond nodded curtly. Ash smudged one of his cheeks like war paint and he still smelled like smoke. "You bet I am. He took everything from me, Luke. Burned my home and killed my best friend. I want to see the son of a bitch up close and personal."

"You and me both." Stone opened the driver's side door. "So let's roll."

Stone had agreed to meet with Blake primarily to set up the tail. He had little interest in negotiating with the man. Blake was a lethal menace and seeing him dead or behind bars was the only acceptable outcome. He knew there were risks associated with meeting the enemy but all he could do was try to minimize the variables and play the cards as they were dealt.

A few miles from town, State Route 3 leveled out as it crossed a narrow plateau between two small mountains. Stone had chosen the spot for the meeting because it was more open than most of the rocky reaches of the Adirondacks and therefore offered less concealment options for an ambush party. He couldn't control how Blake chose to play this, but he did his best to control the environment with the short notice he had been given. It wasn't perfect, but no plan ever was.

Stone glanced over at Drummond. The old guy was made of stern stuff. After all the loss he had suffered, most people would have been curled up in the fetal position, sucking their thumb and wondering why God had pissed all over them. But not Drummond. Here he was, all leather-tough and steely-eyed, ready to saddle up and get the job done. Stone admired the man's grit.

The plateau loomed up ahead. The meeting point was a rest stop the state had built years ago to take advantage of the spectacular views of the smaller mountains nearby and the higher peaks off in the distance.

As Stone swung the Blazer into the pull-off, he saw a black SUV was already parked there, engine idling as exhaust smoke leaked from the tailpipe into the cold, early morning air. The grayness of dawn consumed the sky, rendering the light stale, the sun not yet cresting the eastern ridgelines.

"How do we play this?" Drummond asked. His voice was clear and calm. He had to be seething with a hunger for vengeance, but it didn't show in his tone.

"Blake and I have a chat. You watch my back. Blake will have a guy watching his. Keep your eyes peeled and follow my lead."

"I know you got that Colt in your pocket. You planning on taking him out?"

"Just gonna have a talk and see what happens from there."

"Got it."

Stone parked near a cement picnic table. The Blazer and black SUV were the only two vehicles there. Blake exited his ride, followed by a bodyguard dressed in black from the knit cap on his head to the combat boots on his feet. Stone recognized him as one of the heavies that had tried to stare him down in the courtroom. The guy didn't even try to hide the sidearm slung low in a tactical drop leg holster.

Stone and Blake slowly approached each other, each equally wary, until they met in the middle. Their backup men lingered a dozen paces behind. No morning breeze yet but even if there had been, it would not have been enough to whisk away the hostility that hung thick in the air.

"I didn't think you'd show up." Blake's shaved head was patchy with bristle and gray hairs speckled his goatee. His eyes were dark and malevolent, streaked with cruel amusement. Stone had seen those kind of eyes before and without fail, they belonged to men who delighted in the dispensation of pain and misery.

"You thought wrong," Stone said.

"Let's cut right to the chase." Blake adopted a matter-of-fact tone. "No point in dancing around each other when we both know what I want. Dorey is ours and you're going to give him to us."

"You honestly think you can attack my deputies and assault my station and just get away with it?" Stone shook his head. "I didn't come here to barter with you, Blake. I came here to tell you that I'm going to fuck you up."

"And so it begins." Blake smiled and spread his arms. "Do you know what the United States has become, Stone? A godforsaken cesspool of ragheads and mud people and illegal immigrants and job-stealing wetbacks. Drug dealers and rapists and child molesters from foreign shores. All part of the masterplan of the Jewish overlords running this country. And the government just sits back and lets it happen because all the politicians, every last stinking one of them, are on the fucking take." He paused and the eyes that had seemed so lifeless a few moments ago now blazed with intense hatred. "It's wrong, Stone, and you know it. And patriots like me... well, we can't just stand by anymore. This government *needs* to be overthrown."

"And you think you've got a chance in hell? The

government could wipe you off the face of the earth with a single tactical nuke."

"Not if they can't find us."

Stone kept his face blank as he thought about the State Police helicopter hovering behind a ridge a few miles away, using the rugged terrain and distance as a sound barrier to prevent Blake from detecting its presence. Once The Remnant leader was back in the SUV and on the move, the chopper would swing into action and track him from high above.

Blake continued his speech, his voice strong and assured, confident he held the upper hand.

"America is becoming a wasteland, Stone. Post-apocalyptic, *Mad Max*-type stuff. We're not a republic anymore, we're a collection of neo-feudal states, warring factions with a lust for power, and that lust is the only thing that unites us these days. We all serve different gods while we chase after the same money. And since we have no common purpose anymore we return to the tribal, that most basic unit of humanity. We return to our racial roots because we have to. You're in law enforcement, man, so I know you've seen it play out on prison yards all across America. The Blacks on one side, the Mexicans on the other, and the whites huddled up on whatever square of concrete is left over. It's just the natural order of things. The law of the jungle."

"This country wasn't built on the law of the jungle," Stone said.

"No, America was built on rights – the rights of white people. The founding fathers were slave owners and therefore never intended Blacks to have rights. Only white men. And when those rights are trampled, well, that's what the Second Amendment is for."

"The Second Amendment? That's your justification for shooting a deputy, burning down a house, and attacking my station? Pretty sure that's not what the founders had in mind when they wrote that."

"The founders guaranteed us the pursuit of happiness," said Blake.

"If terrorizing the innocent is your idea of happiness, then you're a mad dog that needs to be put down."

"Fighting for our cause is my happiness, sheriff. This is a war and in war, there are casualties. The primary target of my war is the US government, not your shit-kicker sheriff's department. Hand over Dorey and we'll be on our way, and you won't have any more trouble from us. You have my word."

"Your word doesn't mean a damn thing to me," Stone said. "The answer is no."

"I strongly advise you to reconsider," Blake warned.

"Not gonna happen."

Blake shook his head. "Remember, I tried to be reasonable." He sighed heavily and then stretched, raising his arms above his head.

Stone heard the bullet strike flesh a half-second before he heard the sound of the sniper's shot echo from somewhere up in the nearby mountains.

Drummond went down, making horrible gagging noises, hand clutched to his throat as blood sprayed from between his fingers. He fell to the ground and Stone saw the exit wound; the bullet had torn a lethal chunk out of Drummond's neck.

Even as Stone ran over to his downed deputy, he knew he was too late. Drummond was dead before he even got there.

"You son of a bitch!" Stone roared at Blake. He dug in his coat pocket for the Colt Cobra, but Blake's bodyguard already had the drop on him. The black-clad goon held the semi-automatic pistol in a steady two-handed grip and glared at Stone over the sights, looking like he wanted nothing more in the world than to pull the trigger.

"I have several ex-Special Forces men in my crew," Blake said. "Including one hell of a sniper. You've been in the crosshairs from the moment you rolled up." He pointed at Stone's right pocket. "Take out your peashooter and put it on the ground, nice and slow."

Stone glanced down at the body at his feet. Anger surged through his veins, hot one minute, cold the next, as the need to avenge Drummond's death nearly consumed him and made him think about doing something stupid. A blaze-of-glory desperation play. His hand trembled with the need to pull the gun and start blasting. But he took a deep breath and managed to control it.

Not now, he told himself. *Live to fight another day.*

He took the .38 out of his pocket and dropped it on the ground. He straightened up, pushed back his shoulders, and faced Blake. "Now what?" he growled.

"Now you're going to stay here for the next fifteen minutes," Blake replied. "If you move, my sniper will blow your brains out. Same thing happens if he sees you take your phone out. While you stand here wondering how the hell you fucked this up so badly and how much guilt you should feel for getting your deputy killed, we'll disappear."

Stone said nothing.

"We'll give you three hours to fetch Dorey and bring him here. Leave him at this rest stop. Just drive up, drop him off, and leave. If not, more of your deputies die." Blake turned and headed toward the SUV.

"Hey, Blake."

The Remnant leader paused and looked back over his shoulder. "Yeah?"

"I'm going to kill you."

Blake smiled, thin and cruel, and said, "You can't kill

the devil, Stone." Then he walked to the SUV. Once he was safely inside, his bodyguard backed away, keeping his pistol trained on Stone until the last possible second, then slipping into the vehicle himself.

A moment later, the SUV turned and sped off into the distance.

THIRTY-TWO

STONE SAT ALONE in the sanctuary of the church. The lights were off and the shadows dark, but not nearly as dark as the shadows that clutched his heart. He could feel that need for primal justice prowling around inside him, an angry lion usually caged but now about to be set free to rend and devour. He prayed, not for guidance, but for the strength to return to his warrior ways. Snippets of scripture flickered through his mind. Perhaps answers to his prayers, perhaps just dredged up justifications. Truthfully, he didn't much care which right now.

Blessed be the Lord, my rock, who teaches my hands to war…

The Remnant had shot Valentine. Murdered Drummond. Burned down his home. Attacked the sheriff's station. They lived by an evil, genocidal creed. The whole wicked lot of them deserved to be crushed like bugs under boot heels.

You are my hammer, my weapon of war…

It was time to end this for good. Blake had called himself the devil. Time to send him to hell.

Touch the mountains, so that they smoke…

Stone rose from the pew and headed for the door, leaving this holy place behind as he entered the killing fields once again.

The air unit confirmed that in the aftermath of Drummond's murder, Blake's SUV returned to the forest location of the Hermetic Institute. Stone arranged for units from Milford PD and the State Police to meet him at a staging area a few miles east of the compound, ready to launch an assault.

Stone drove fast, eyes focused on the road ahead while his mind prepared for war. He was ready to kick down doors and put bullets into bad guys. Some men just needed to be wiped off the face of the earth. The Remnant was loaded with such men. Now that Stone had managed to pin down their location, it was time to go in for the kill.

The staging area was the parking lot of an abandoned country store that some hopeful soul had built back in the '80s, hoping to draw in customers commuting between the tri-lakes and Plattsburgh. The place had gone belly-up in less than five years and the building had been suffering a slow-rot death ever since.

Bester and Spencer were already onsite when Stone arrived. Bester stood next to a dilapidated pair of rusting gas pumps with her hands on her hips and a look of real concern on her face as Stone parked the Blazer and approached.

"Sorry about Drummond." She reached out and squeezed his shoulder. "We're gonna nail the bastards who did it."

"From your lips to God's ears." Stone felt the darkness coiled within him, ready to unleash violence. He still struggled to reconcile that darkness with the preacher side of his personality, but it was not a struggle that would keep him from doing what he believed needed to be done.

"Sheriff." Spencer trotted over. "We're ready to go. I've got SWAT boys covering the woods at the rear and sides of the compound. We sent a drone over the property and the intel shows that they've been loading stuff into black SUVs by the main gate for the past forty minutes. Looks like they're getting ready to bug out, so we should hit 'em before they move."

"Right," said Bester. "We hit them now and they're vulnerable. Simple, straight-forward assault."

"Works for me," Stone replied. "Let's roll."

They sped down the road in formation: two police APCs up front, followed by three black SUVs for state and FBI personnel, and a van containing the lead SWAT team.

"We're one minute out," Spencer announced from the passenger seat without turning, keeping his eyes fixed on the road ahead.

Stone's phone buzzed. Sanchez calling from the station. She knew where he was and what he was doing and wouldn't have bothered him if it wasn't important. He pressed the button to accept the call. "What is it, Sanchez?"

"Sir, you know the old warehouse out by the grain feeder silo? By the old railroad tracks?"

"What about it?"

Spencer said, "Thirty seconds."

"Sir, it's all locked up with new chains and padlock."

Something cold swept through Stone. It was a damn good bet that he now knew where the black SUVs had disappeared to after the attack on the station.

Spencer held up one finger, then five, letting Stone know they were fifteen seconds away from contact.

"Put a unit on that building and watch it," Stone ordered. "I'll be in touch." He hung up.

The fence surrounding the Hermetic Institute appeared in the trees up ahead. Chain link, nine feet high, topped with razor wire. Good enough to keep out your average trespasser or lost hiker, but woefully inadequate against a team of professional breachers.

Stone could see the gate and the scattering of SUVs parked nearby with their doors open. Men hustled back and forth between the buildings and vehicles, loading cargo into the hatches.

The lead APC accelerated for the final approach. It smashed into the gate, throwing it open with a screech of twisting metal. Men dropped their boxes and scattered to get out of the way. Almost immediately, weapons appeared in their hands and gunfire crackled at the incoming vehicles.

Spencer barked into the radio, ordering the SWAT teams to move in. They would ghost out of the woods surrounding the property, cut through the fence, and deal with any Remnant members they intercepted.

The SUV carrying Stone, Bester, and Spencer skidded through a drifting half-turn so that the passenger side faced the compound. They all piled out the driver's side. Stone drew his Glock the second his feet touched ground. Beside him, Bester hauled out her .44 Auto Mag.

Spencer shook his head. "I can't believe you brought that hand cannon."

"Just taking Teddy Roosevelt's advice," Bester replied. "Speak softly and carry big-ass artillery."

The SWAT team deployed in a well-disciplined line behind the armored vehicles. The Remnant members crouched behind their SUVs and opened fire in a furious volley. SWAT poured it right back at them. Two enemy combatants went down, one with a hole drilled through his heart, the other with the top of his head peeled off.

Trusting SWAT to handle the frontal assault, Stone and Bester ducked into the trees and followed the fence line to the north. A few stray shots sizzled their way, tearing ragged splinters from the tree trunks, but for the most part the SWAT team kept The Remnant soldiers occupied.

They found themselves behind a set of utility buildings. Air-cooling units hummed, barely audible over the sound of gunfire at the front gate. Plastic garbage bins perched in orderly rows. Stone threaded his way through them, covered by Bester, until he could peer around the edge of the structure.

"What's the plan?" she asked.

"Find Blake," Stone replied, making it sound so simple. The firefight at the front gate reached a crescendo then died down for a moment. As if picking up the slack, a flurry of shots rang out from the rear of the compound, presumably the secondary SWAT team making contact with the enemy. "He's got to be here somewhere."

"I'm guessing he's not a lead-from-the-front kind of guy," Bester said. "Probably hole up while the fighting is going down."

Stone pointed at a large Quonset hut in the center of the compound. It seemed curiously still despite the chaos raging all around it. "The bigger the building, the more places to hide," he said. "Maybe he's in there."

"So let's go knock on the door." Bester hefted her Auto Mag.

"Can't hurt to try."

"He shoots you, it'll hurt like hell."

"Point taken."

They quickly crossed the open ground until they were pressed up against the wall of the Quonset hut. They crouched low as a truck sped past, carrying Remnant reinforcements to the front gate. Looked like the bastards intended to put up a fight.

"Think this is their ops center?" Bester asked.

"I'm thinking that if they've got an arms pipeline coming from the military base, they need somewhere to store it, and this place looks big enough to do the job."

"Damn place is big enough to be an aircraft hangar," Bester muttered. It would be another few moments before she realized the accuracy of her words.

Down at the far end, a wide door set on rails started to slide open. Stone and Bester hugged the wall as a crew of three men wearing black jumpsuits wheeled out an aircraft that resembled a giant mechanical dragonfly.

"Holy shit," Bester breathed. "Is that a fucking helicopter?"

"Yeah." Stone studied the machine. It was a Mosquito XET, a single-seat, personal use, ultralight chopper. Last time he had seen one had been on a corrupt billionaire's estate in Monaco. By the time Stone left, the billionaire didn't need it anymore. Hard to fly Mosquitoes in hell.

As they watched, Blake appeared with a backpack slung over his shoulder. He boarded the mini copter and started poring over the instruments.

"Stand back." Bester raised her Auto Mag. "With a little luck, I can blow out the engine from here."

Stone knew Bester's hand cannon would send a .44 caliber bullet downrange at 1,800 feet per second. Her target was the silver-colored turbine housing on the Mosquito. Put a round or two in there and the result would be twisted, mangled metal that would prevent the aircraft from taking off. But they were far enough away that a hit wasn't guaranteed, not with a handgun.

"Blow the engine? I'd rather you blew his head off," Stone growled.

"I'm a law enforcement officer," Bester replied. "Not a killer."

Before Stone could say anything else, she stepped away from the wall and lined up the chopper in her sights. But as she did so, one of the crew members spotted her.

"Hey!" the man yelled, clawing for the pistol holstered on his belt.

Bester shifted her aim, pulled the trigger, and blew the guy's head into a smoking ruin.

Stone's lips peeled back from his teeth in a mirthless grin. "You were saying?"

"Shut up."

Stone dropped to one knee and bracketed Blake in the gunsights of his Glock. The Remnant leader remained cool under fire. Instead of panicking, he worked on the controls. The rotors began to turn.

Bester's Auto Mag roared again. A chunk of the chopper's body work tore away but it wasn't a crippling blow. Bester cursed and repositioned herself as the rotors gained speed.

Stone took his shot.

Just as the trigger reached breakpoint, the chopper lurched into the air. The bullet that would have punched clean through Blake's heart instead ripped into his thigh. Blake slapped a hand over the bloody wound. From this far away, Stone couldn't actually see the look of pain on Blake's face but he damn sure imagined it.

Stone rose from his crouch and powered forward, Glock raised. He needed to close the gap and get a high-percentage shot at the bastard.

He made it two steps before another crew member charged out of the hangar space brandishing an assault rifle, the weapon already spitting lead. Stone dove to the side, narrowly avoiding the blast of full-auto fire. Bullets sizzled through the space he had occupied a split second before.

He landed hard on his shoulder and used his momentum to roll up onto one knee, pistol hunting for a target. Another salvo smashed into the ground in front of him, tearing up divots and hurling chunks of frozen dirt into his face.

Half-blinded, he saw the mini chopper crest the tree-tops and bank southeast, back in the direction of Whisper Falls. Clearly Blake's thigh wound had not incapacitated his ability to fly the aircraft. Stone felt gut punched as the Mosquito disappeared. He couldn't believe Blake had just escaped the clutches of justice.

He forced the bitter thought aside. Right now he needed to focus on his current vulnerability. He was kneeling in the dirt with no cover, a good way to get dead. The Remnant gunner had missed twice. Stone doubted he would miss a third time.

He threw himself to the side as the gunman's assault rifle rattled to life again, steeling himself for the burning pain of hot lead ripping into his flesh. Bullets chased him across the ground as he rolled desperately.

This is it, he thought. *I'm a goner.*

Then Bester's Auto Mag roared and the gunman's head vaporized into a red mist.

Stone climbed to his feet as Bester ordered the sole survivor to put his hands on his head and get on his knees. But the guy chose to die free rather than face prison bars. Snarling obscenities and racial epithets, he raised his pistol and charged them both in a suicide play.

Stone's Glock and Bester's Auto Mag roared at the

same time, blowing a pair of holes through the man's chest. Heart and lungs a mangled mess, the guy was dead before he hit the ground.

Stone brushed the dirt off his coat and pants. As he did so, he noticed that the sound of gunfire from other parts of the compound had died down.

"No more gunshots," Bester said, echoing his thoughts. "Looks like we've secured the place."

"Thought that guy was gonna nail me," Stone said. "Thanks for saving my ass."

"No problem. It's a nice enough ass, if I was into straight guys' asses." Bester winked at him.

Stone grinned and shook his head. Together they walked over and looked inside the Quonset hut.

Whatever had been stored here was now long gone. Stone suspected the same would be true of the other buildings dotting the grounds. They would scour everything for clues to what The Remnant was up to, but Stone didn't hold out much hope of finding any answers.

He raised his eyes and watched the chopper become a distant speck in the winter sky.

———

"How many?"

"We arrested fifteen." Spencer pointed to where the police had The Remnant members corralled near the front gate, hands cuffed behind them as they sat on the ground under the watchful eyes of SWAT team members. "Four wounded, plus three killed, not counting the three that you and Bester zapped."

"None of which were Blake, that son of a bitch."

Spencer slapped him on the shoulder. "We'll get him, don't worry."

Stone's phone vibrated in his pocket. He pulled it out,

saw that it was the station trying to reach him, and answered the call. "This is Stone."

"Sir, it's Sanchez." She talked fast, the words coming out in a rush. "You need to get back here ASAP."

"What's wrong?"

"A chopper just landed out by the old grain feeder silo and then a bunch of tractor trailers and SUVs came barreling out of the old warehouse."

"Anybody see where they headed?"

"They're here, sir."

"What do you mean?"

"They're at the station, sir. They surrounded us. Used the trucks to block us off on all sides and set up an armed perimeter. They've got a small army."

Stone clenched his teeth so hard that his jaw started to ache.

"Sir?" Sanchez couldn't quite keep the tremor out of her voice. "We're trapped."

THIRTY-THREE

"YOU KNOW *the old warehouse out by the grain feeder silo? By the old railroad tracks? It's all locked up with new chains and padlock."*

It was all starting to make sense. The SUVs, the smuggled arms shipments, the missing Cardine trucks...The Remnant had hidden them in the abandoned warehouse by the old railyard, right under their noses. Hell, they had most likely even stashed some of their soldiers there to guard the supplies.

"Hold 'em off. Shoot to kill if you have to," Stone said to Sanchez. "We're on our way." He hung up the phone and turned to Bester. "Blake just landed back in town. He's got the station house surrounded."

"Let's go." Bester dashed for the FBI SUV at a dead run, Stone right on her heels. She had the engine revving two seconds after they jumped in the vehicle.

"Thought this was a sleepy little town, Stone." Bester spun the wheel and punched the gas, whipping the SUV around so that they were racing back down the road toward Whisper Falls.

"We have our moments."

"Quiet little mountain town with an honest-to-God cowboy for a sheriff. Sounds downright bucolic." Bester hit the lights and sirens as they roared down Route 3. "Until you factor in the neo-Nazi terrorists."

"Nothing that bullets in their brainpans won't solve," Stone said grimly.

Bester dodged around a slow-moving logging truck. Her speed was reckless, but Stone wasn't complaining. He had deputies in grave danger and he needed to get there fast, caution be damned. He kept his men trained as best he could, but they were still just small-town cops going up against tactically-proficient operators. Without backup, they would be cut down in short order.

"This Blake bastard is a real pain in the ass," Bester growled as the SUV chewed up the miles. "He's starting to get on my goddamned nerves." She jerked the wheel to the left and slalomed around a morning commuter.

"Any chance the FBI can send more agents?" Stone asked.

"What's the matter? One psycho lesbian SSA with a handgun fetish isn't enough for you?"

"I never said you were psycho."

Bester's lips twitched in a quick, crooked grin.

Stone's guts churned with anger as he stared out the window, watching the rugged landscape whip by as he worried about his deputies trapped in the station. It was past time to bury Blake under six feet of cold, hard dirt.

"You gotta hand it to Blake," Bester said. "The guy's got ambition."

"What he's got is a bullet with his name on it," Stone rasped.

Bester shot him a sideways glance. "You're one weird preacher, Stone."

He didn't reply, but she wasn't wrong. Right now, hungry for a man's blood, Stone didn't feel like much of a preacher at all. It bothered him on some level but not enough to rein in his killer impulses. Whatever light existed within him had been swallowed by the dark need for vengeance.

In the driver's seat, Bester seemed coiled with tension. They had narrowly survived the assault on the compound and now they were getting ready to jump right back into a life-or-death confrontation. Stone's warrior days had steeled his nerves to bullets and blood. He wasn't so sure about Bester.

His driveway appeared up ahead. Stone pointed at the turnoff. "Drop me off here."

"Your house? Are you kidding?"

"I need to grab some gear."

"What kind of gear?"

"The full-auto kind. I'll meet you at the station."

"How?" Bester looked puzzled but obediently pulled into the driveway. "Your Blazer is in town."

"I'm going old school."

———

Stone saddled Rocky with the kind of speed that comes from years of horseback riding. He then hurried down to the basement and opened his gun vault.

He selected an HK416 submachine gun, one sporting a suppressor, looping the sling over his shoulder so that the rifle hung across his back. Several handguns, grenades, and ammunition went into a backpack. Lastly, he grabbed the Seekins Precision Havok Pro .338 rifle before heading back upstairs.

Tied to a fence post out back, Rocky snorted and stamped his hooves as Stone approached, seeming to recognize that something was up.

"Time for war, hoss." Stone loaded the backpack into

one of the saddlebags. "Got some bad men out there that need killing." He slid the Seekins into a scabbard.

The Appaloosa stallion gave him a look that showed no fear. Stone patted him on the neck. This horse was game for anything.

Stone swung up into the saddle and they headed for town at a full gallop. Rocky's hooves flung clods of frozen dirt into the air as they raced through the woods that would bring them to the backside of Whisper Falls.

———

The terrain between the parsonage and Whisper Falls was hilly and wooded. Stone had never ridden it before, but he had hiked through there a few times. No official trails; just game paths created by the snowshoe hares, foxes, coy wolves, whitetail deer, and black bears that populated the region.

He kept the reins loose, giving Rocky his head, trusting the horse to find the best way through the forest. The stallion slowed down from a full-on gallop as the woods thickened but still maintained a fast canter without needing to be spurred along by Stone. The Appaloosa seemed to sense the urgency of the mission and kept his feet moving as quickly as possible over the snow-covered ground.

Stone stayed alert for low branches. Last thing he needed right now was to catch a limb in the face and get peeled out of the saddle. He clamped his Stetson down tight on his head and stayed low over Rocky's neck, watching their progress from between the stallion's pricked-forward ears.

Going on horseback would allow him to sneak into the backside of Whisper Falls, keeping to the thick forest that surrounded the town. Unless he had underestimated them, The Remnant would be watching for him to arrive on four wheels, not four legs.

His plan was to access the besieged sheriff's station through the back door. The building sat at the bottom of a steep, wooded hill, just on the other side of a shallow ravine. The Saranac River threaded through the bottom of the gully, narrowing to a pinch point that was only twenty yards across but boiling with rapids. White water churned and foamed over the rocks.

A few years back, the town had constructed the River-walk, a brick pathway that ran alongside the river as it flowed through the heart of Whisper Falls. The Riverwalk began – or concluded, depending on which end you started at – behind the sheriff's station, a wooden foot-bridge traversing the ravine so people could lean over the railing and watch the rapids below.

There was a small lot behind the station, used primarily to secure confiscated vehicles and patrol cars waiting for repairs, separated from the Riverwalk by a simple chain-link fence with a padlocked gate. The lot was far too small to accommodate a tractor trailer and the ravine served as a natural barrier.

Since there was no way to barricade the back of the station with one of the Cardine trucks, Stone expected it to be the weakest part of the blockade. No doubt it would be guarded, but not at the same strength-level as the front and sides. It would be the best place to penetrate The Remnant's perimeter.

When they neared town, he put a firmer hand on the reins to circle Rocky behind the high school and into the woods there. He guided the stallion to the crest of the hill overlooking the sheriff's station and dismounted, hitching the horse to a maple tree.

As he gathered up his weapons, he became aware of the ominous silence. Not just here in the woods, but the town in general. Given the lethal threat now surrounding the sheriff's station, Stone had no doubt that traffic had been diverted, schools placed on lockdown, citizens ordered to vacate the area or shelter in place. The Remnant had invaded Whisper Falls and it royally pissed Stone off.

The slope facing the sheriff's office was lush with pines, offering choice concealment as Stone picked his way down the hill. He ghosted from tree to tree, creeping lower, until he could hear the liquid roar of the rapids. The fast-moving water never froze, even in the dead of winter.

He edged forward another few meters, ducking beneath some snow-laden pine boughs. From this vantage point, peering out from between gaps in the branches, he could see the back of the station.

His guess had paid off. There were no trucks back there, just a couple of Honda four-wheelers parked nose-to-nose in front of the gate, manned by a pair of Remnant gunmen.

Stone dropped to one knee and braced the muzzle of the HK416 against the trunk of the tree he was using for cover. He calculated the range at just under 200 meters, well within the rifle's capabilities, especially with a seasoned shooter on the trigger. The suppressor would ensure the shots weren't loud enough to alert Blake and his Remnant army that their rear guard had been taken out.

He briefly thought of Bester. He hoped she was out there somewhere, rallying a hard-charging response to Blake's bold, brash, ballsy move. Then he spared a thought for Holly, the woman who mattered most to him in this world. He prayed when this was all over, he was still alive to see her again.

Then he pushed them both out of his mind. Right now

there was another woman he needed to talk to. He took out his cell phone and dialed a number.

She answered on the second ring. "This is Sanchez."

"It's Stone." He kept his voice low, wanting to make sure it wouldn't carry down the hill, even though he was pretty confident the rushing water would mask any sound short of a bull moose bellowing. "I'll be coming in the back door in a minute. Make sure it's not locked."

"It's good to hear your voice, sir." Sanchez sounded relieved. "But the back door is guarded."

"Not for long."

"Understood. I'll meet you there."

"Make sure the coffee's hot." Stone hung up and dropped the phone back in his pocket before settling down behind the gunsights again. He figured two quick shots to take out the sentries, run down the hill and across the bridge, another bullet to crack open the padlock, and a short dash inside the station. Start to finish, just under a minute, give or take.

As long as nothing went wrong.

He closed his left eye and settled the HK's sights on the head of The Remnant soldier to his left. He could swing a gun from left to right faster than he could right to left. The time difference wasn't much, but right now, slivers of seconds counted.

The target never felt the bullet that killed him. Stone's shot drilled him right between the eyes, scrambled his brains, and blew them out the back of his skull.

The other soldier barely had time to grasp his partner's death before he joined him. Stone's second bullet burrowed through the man's ribcage and blasted into his heart. The high-powered impacts kicked both men off their four-wheelers like scarecrows struck by a wrecking ball. They sprawled unceremoniously on the blood-splattered ground.

Stone thought that he should feel remorse but it just wasn't there. Sometimes evil just deserved to die. Maybe when this was over, he would feel something. Or maybe he would just keep on suppressing his conscience until his soul was nothing but a patchwork of scars.

He shoved aside the introspection at the same time he pushed through the pine branches and ran down the hill toward the ravine. He ducked and weaved in a random, zigzagging pattern in case unseen shooters tried to put him in the crosshairs. He tripped over a rock hidden under the snowpack and almost went down but managed to keep his balance.

He reached the bottom of the hill and his boots thudded on the wooden boards of the footbridge. Out here in the open, he felt horribly exposed and crossed the bridge as fast as he could.

On the other side, he pumped a bullet into the padlock on the gate, scrambling it into scrap metal. He stepped over the two corpses sprawled beside their ATVs, pushed through the gate, and ran toward the back door of the sheriff's station.

He grabbed the handle and tried to open it.

Locked.

Shit!

He tried again, rattling the doorknob as hard as he could.

Nothing.

He hissed a curse through clenched teeth. Where the hell was Sanchez?

Two Remnant soldiers chose that moment to come around the corner of the building. They had assault rifles in their hands with the muzzles pointed at the ground. The direction of the muzzles quickly changed when they saw their dead comrades lying next to the four-wheelers. They snapped the rifles up to their shoulders as their eyes looked for the threat. A half-heartbeat later they spotted Stone standing by the door.

That half-heartbeat cost them their lives.

Stone whipped his HK through a tight figure-eight pattern. The bullets stitched the duo across their upper and lower torsos, tearing apart flesh and bone, exploding the vitals beneath.

As the two targets toppled to the ground, the door swung open. Sanchez stood there, a set of keys in her left hand, a Glock pistol in her right. "Been waiting long?" she asked.

Stone hauled himself through the doorway and Sanchez secured it behind him. "Long enough to add a couple more to my kill count."

"That's just an appetizer. Get ready for the main course."

Just then, a hail of gunfire sounded from the front of the building.

THIRTY-FOUR

STONE RAN DOWN THE HALL, carrying the extra rifles and gear. Sanchez followed hot on his heels.

The front area of the office was still in ruins from The Remnant's attack last night. The deputies had done a quick cleanup but there'd been no time to get it all. Glass and debris crunched under their boots. The tarp hanging over the blown-out windows had been shredded by auto-fire and now hung in ragged streamers, twisting in the wind like blue-vinyl ghosts. Gun smoke drifted in from outside.

Stone positioned himself next to the front window. The other on-duty deputies hunkered down behind desks and filing cabinets. The gunfire slackened, then stopped. Probably just a random, fire-for-effect salvo to keep their heads down. But Stone had no doubt that before too long, Blake and his boys would stop wasting time with pot-shots and make a serious attempt to breach the station.

Stone peered between gaps in the tarp. He saw a tractor trailer blocking the front of the building.

"There's five trucks total," Sanchez reported. "The one

out front and two on each side. Nothing out back, as you know."

"They might not know the back is unguarded yet," Stone said. "Anyone wants to slip out the back door, now's the time."

"Retreat?" Sanchez made it sound like an obscenity. "From the gutless bastards who shot Valentine and killed Drummond? Not a chance in hell, sir." The other deputies nodded their heads in agreement.

"Fair enough," Stone said. "Forget I mentioned it."

"I've got Catfish up on the roof," Sanchez said. "He's keeping them from moving around too much."

Stone nodded. That was good news. Abe 'Catfish' Lewis was the best sniper in the Adirondacks, a Louisiana transplant who had traded the bayous for the high peaks.

"Here." Stone opened the backpack. "I brought more ammo, a couple extra pistols, and some grenades."

Sanchez's eyes widened. "Looks like Christmas came early."

Stone pocketed three of the grenades for himself and then handed her the rest of the hardware, along with the HK416. "Pass these out as you see fit. I'm heading up to the roof."

"Don't get killed."

"Not planning on it, but shit happens."

Stone picked up the Seekins and made his way to the maintenance room in the rear section of the building. There wasn't much in there; just a slop sink, an old locker that boasted more rust than paint, and a janitorial cart stacked with cleaning supplies. In the corner, a steel ladder led up to the roof. Stone slung the Seekins over his shoulder, grabbed the rungs, and started climbing.

The access hatch was heavy and stubborn, but he got it open. He stayed low as he exited onto the roof, not wanting to silhouette himself against the sky and give The Remnant gunners a tempting target.

Catfish glanced at him, his bearded face creased in a lopsided grin despite the dangerous circumstances. "Howdy, boss," he said in his laid back, Cajun-accented drawl. "The sons of bitches are still out there."

"Got a head count?"

"Nothing more than a wild-ass guess, but it looks like they got about forty guys. They're scuttling around behind those big-ass trucks like beetles in a dung pile so it's hard to get a bead on 'em, but I did manage to perforate one of 'em." He gestured vaguely off to his right.

Keeping low, Stone glanced over the edge of the roof. Crumpled lifelessly in a wide pool of blood next to one of the rigs was a corpse with a gaping, center-mass hole in its chest.

"Good shooting, Cat." Stone studied the rest of the scene. The sheriff's station was small and the tractor trailers had them boxed in tightly. The gaps between the trucks were just wide enough for a man to navigate, which allowed them to step out, fire their shots, and instantly retreat back behind the cover of the rigs. Black SUVs had also been strategically arranged on the far side of the tractor trailers to provide cover and concealment.

Several hundred yards away, on the other side of Wildflower Avenue, it looked like Bester had posted up in the parking lot of a bakery along with the State Police and deputies who had participated in the raid earlier. But there weren't enough of them to overrun The Remnant's barricaded position.

Stone took out his phone and made a call.

She answered on the first ring. "Bester."

"It's Stone."

"My favorite cowboy."

"More like the only cowboy you know."

"Which makes you my favorite."

"I made it inside. I'm on the roof. Got a handful of deputies holding the fort downstairs. What's your status?"

"I made some calls and asked for the National Guard to be deployed, but still waiting for a decision. Could be another hour, maybe more."

"We don't have an hour." Stone lowered the phone and looked at Catfish. "We still got Dorey locked up?"

"Yup. The sorry cuss is moping in his cell, whining about some deal you supposedly made with him."

"Good." Stone put the phone back up to his ear and said to Bester, "We've still got Dorey in lockup. That's why they're here. They want us to let him go."

"Do they really think they can get away with this?" Bester's voice sounded volcanic, even over the phone.

"Sure as hell looks like they're gonna try," Stone said.

"And we're the unlucky ones who get to stand in their way."

"You can tuck tail and run if you want."

"Kiss my ass, cowboy! I've got just as much heart as you and double the balls. I'll outdrink you, out-fuck you, and outfight you on your best night."

"That's the spirit. Let's kick the shit out of these guys."

"Copy that, Stone. See you on the other side."

Stone hung up, put the phone in his pocket, and pulled out a grenade. He looked at Catfish. "Time to let these bastards know we came to play."

"Gonna give 'em a bit of the ol' boom-boom?"

"You know it."

Stone pulled the pin. As he fast pitched the grenade down at the vehicular barricade, Catfish banged out a pair of shots to provide cover.

The grenade flew through the air, hit the ground,

and bounced between two rigs. A shout of alarm was cut off by the ear-rupturing blast. A Remnant soldier launched through the air like a shredded scarecrow, clothes charred and smoking. He landed on the sidewalk with blood pouring from the lethal shrapnel wounds.

Before the explosion even ebbed, Catfish fired more rounds down at the trucks. His bullets shattered windshields and punched holes in bodywork. Far as Stone could tell, none of them struck flesh, but that was okay. Right now, they were just reminding The Remnant that they wouldn't go down without a fight.

"Yeehaw!" Catfish howled and punched his fist in the air. He then threw his rifle back up to his shoulder and snapped off a shot that tore open the front tire of a truck. "That hauler ain't goin' nowhere!" he shouted, then laughed maniacally.

"Hey, Cat?" Stone gave him a sidelong glance. "How many tours did you do in Afghanistan?"

"Four, boss. Best years of my life, playin' in the sandbox."

"You should probably talk to somebody."

"I went to that shrink you recommended. She told me to stop coming after the third session." Catfish grinned. "Said I made her feel unsafe."

Shaking his head, Stone scanned the street below again. He detected movement behind the tractor trailers, fleeting glimpses of bodies in motion through the gaps between the trucks.

"They'll make a move soon," he said to Catfish. "I'm going back down and check on the others. Those bastards start any shit, rain fire down on their heads. I'll be back in a few minutes." He took the two grenades from his pocket and set them on the edge of the roof. "At your discretion."

"Guns and grenades? This is the best birthday ever!" Catfish exclaimed.

"Is it really your birthday?" Stone asked.

"Yep."

Stone shook his head again. "Talk about one hell of a Happy Birthday."

————

Stone dropped back down through the roof hatch to the main floor. Sanchez had posted a deputy at the rear door while the rest covered the front. More filing cabinets and boxes of copier paper had been stacked in front of the blown-out windows. Not exactly Fort Apache but the best they could do under the circumstances.

They all looked at him, waiting for his words, some kind of rallying cry. He found himself wondering how many of them would survive the coming battle, but quickly shook it off. Dwelling on death wouldn't help anything right now.

"Unless I'm behind a pulpit, I'm not much for speeches," he said. "I'm guessing those sons of bitches outside will make their move pretty soon. They believe they can come in here and take what they want. But we're going to show them they're wrong. *Dead* wrong. Make no mistake, this is gonna be a kill-or-be-killed kind of fight."

He paused and took the time to look each of them in the eye before he spoke again.

"We could just give them Dorey and call it a day. But that's not the oath we took. If we're not ready to die in the name of justice, then we don't deserve to wear the badge."

"Damn straight," Sanchez said, and the other deputies nodded.

"Give them the fight of their lives," Stone said. "Make

them eat bullets. Make them earn every inch of ground. No fighting pretty; this is the law of the jungle. Watch your six, make your shots count, and get ready to send these bastards to hell."

Without another word, Stone turned and walked back to the ladder to rejoin Catfish on the roof.

"Damn," one of the deputies muttered. "Thought he said he sucked at speeches."

THIRTY-FIVE

A FEW MINUTES LATER, Blake stepped out from between two trucks. He had a slight limp, most likely from the bullet wound in his thigh Stone had given him earlier. He also had a handkerchief in his fist and waved it like a white flag as he stared up at the roof. The smirking grin on the man's face annoyed Stone.

"Looks like our resident alpha-Nazi asshole wants to chat." Catfish pointed with his middle finger. "Want me to shoot him in the nuts?"

"Keep the crosshairs on him but don't pull the trigger just yet." Stone peered over the edge of the roof at the man standing beneath his symbol of temporary truce. "What do you want, Blake?"

"You know exactly what I want." Blake's grin turned wolfish. "I'm giving you one chance to give us Dorey before we come in there and take him. And Stone, if you make us do that, it'll be shoot to kill, take-no-prisoners time. Look around, man. You're outnumbered and we've got the superior firepower. Do the right thing, send Dorey out, and nobody else has to die."

"Wrong," Stone rasped. "There's somebody else that

needs to die. You've killed too many people for me to just let you walk away."

"I'm a soldier, Stone, and soldiers kill for their cause."

Stone's mouth twisted in contempt. Listening to this murderer call himself a soldier was an insult to the true soldiers Stone had served with back in his warrior days.

He stared at Blake. The man had come from a business background – a world of negotiations, equivocations, and manipulations – but had decided to remake himself as a soldier. He had mastered the outward, physical aspects, and even familiarized himself with tactical basics.

But what he lacked were the internal resources. Things that couldn't be taught. Things like resolve, moral discipline, and honor. And lacking a noble cause that truly mattered, he cloaked himself in a false flag that preached hate and justified the violence he longed to unleash.

In the end, Blake was nothing more than a wannabe playing at being a soldier.

Some men died for a righteous cause. Stone intended to make Blake die for his unrighteous one.

"I made you a reservation in hell," Stone growled. "Don't be late."

Blake's grin widened and curved like a sickle as he pointed up at Stone – "See you soon, sheriff." – and stepped back behind the trucks.

————

"Looks like they're getting ready to move," said Bester.

Stone held the phone to his ear as he stared down at The Remnant forces. "We figured they'd make their play long before the National Guard got here."

"From my angle, looks like Blake is holding a small

defensive group in reserve to keep us from flanking his rear."

"Will it work?"

"Only one way to find out," Bester replied. "I'm damn sure not going to just sit here twiddling my thumbs while these bastards attempt to take down a sheriff's department. I've got a few of your deputies here, along with some state boys. When Blake makes his move, we'll launch a counterassault right up his backside. You give 'em hell from the front and we'll bring the pain from the rear."

"Let's hope it's enough."

"You're a preacher," Bester said. "Getting by on a hope and a prayer is kind of your thing."

Next to Stone, Catfish muttered, "They're on the move. Suckers are scurrying around like cockroaches in the light."

Stone nodded. Through the narrow gaps, he glimpsed a lot of movement behind the trucks. Looked like Blake and his soldiers were preparing to penetrate.

Not if I've got anything to say about it, he thought grimly.

To Bester, he said, "Game time."

"See you on the other side, cowboy. Stay alive and the first drink is on me."

Stone hung up and put the phone back in his pocket. He brought the Seekins to his shoulder and trained the scope on one of the gaps between the trucks. First man to make the mistake of entering his crosshairs was going down. That would send a message to the others that they might pay a deadly price for their actions.

Down among The Remnant ranks, someone whistled and black-clad fascists moved into the gaps. They ducked low in combat crouches as they rushed the station.

Stone clenched his jaw. It was killing time.

He fired a shot, rode out the recoil, and watched the target's head split wide open. The man fell to the ground with his cranial contents evacuated, brain muck spattering the men behind him. They quickly dragged his corpse out of sight.

One floor down, Sanchez and the other deputies fired a ragged volley down on The Remnant as they stormed forward.

Catfish joined the action, hurling wildly profane insults even faster than bullets.

Remnant soldiers dropped, but not enough to freeze the attack. They kept pouring through the gaps, assault rifles snapping off cover fire in a harsh, staccato rhythm.

Three men rushed forward and hurled Molotov cocktails at the front of the station. Mostly brick and glass, there was little to burn, but the flash-fired gasoline set flame to the tarps covering the broken windows.

Risking a glance over the edge of the roof, Stone glimpsed fire racing up the nylon material. Within moments, the front windows of the station became a sheet of flames. Sanchez and the deputies were not only blinded, but unable to fire at the invaders.

Which, Stone realized, was exactly The Remnant's tactical plan.

He fired another shot from his rifle and took off the top of a man's skull, dropping him in a heap on the ground.

Beside him, Catfish cranked off a pair of shots and two more men went down. Gunfire crackled from the main floor of the station. Sanchez and his deputies might not be able to see out the windows but they were still sending rounds downrange, firing blind at the attacking Remnant forces.

Catfish touched Stone's shoulder and pointed.

Stone swiveled his head and saw a four-man assault

team creeping around the front of the tractor trailer to their left. He swung his rifle toward them, and Catfish did the same. Stone hoped Blake was among them but when he got them in his scope, he didn't recognize any of their faces.

"Damn it, Blake, where are you?" he growled softly.

"Hiding in the back like a gutless sissy," Catfish said. "He'll wait until it's over and then rush in to claim the glory."

"He's not claiming anything but a cheap coffin and a shallow grave." Stone racked his rifle bolt. "You take the ones on the left, I'll take the right."

"You betcha."

Both men opened fire. Stone's bullets sent two of them flipping backward while Catfish's slugs tore apart the chests of the other two.

"Them boys ain't got no heart," Catfish said, and Stone couldn't tell if he was cracking a joke or not.

Looking out over the trucks, Stone saw Bester and her troops pushing forward. The Remnant's rear defense snapped some shots in their direction but there weren't enough of them to hold back the assault team. Blake had left his rear flank stretched too thin, the bulk of his forces committed to breaching the sheriff's station and breaking out Dorey.

Below, Sanchez and the deputies continued to send bullets ripping blindly through the burning tarps. Stone heard one of the HKs cutting loose on full-auto. He saw another Remnant soldier tumble to the ground with a line of blood-spurting holes stitched across his torso.

The enemy wave rushed forward, picking up speed. Stone acquired a target in his sniper scope and put him down. Catfish added another one to his kill count as well.

"God, I love this dance." The deputy's ear-to-ear grin made him look happier than a little kid hopped up on

Halloween candy. He fired again and turned a soldier's skull to mush. The guy dropped to the ground like a string-cut puppet.

Bester's troops were in a full-fledged clash with The Remnant rear guard. Gunfire roared in a violent symphony, the screams of the wounded and dying adding to the chaotic soundscape. The surviving Remnant gunmen began backing up, giving up ground, and turned toward the sheriff's station. With their rear position cut off, the only way out now was forward.

"You good?" Stone asked Catfish. "I'm going back down and check on the others."

"Good? This is more fun than shootin' swamp gators!"

Stone climbed back down the ladder and found Sanchez.

"They're coming," he said, loud enough for all the deputies to hear. "They've got the numbers to make it inside, so get ready for an up close and personal fight."

Every man double-checked his weapons and performed tactical magazine exchanges where necessary, making sure they were topped off with maximum bullet capacity.

Stone leaned against a filing cabinet and took several deep breaths. Soon, he thought. One way or the other, it would all be over soon.

Those few seconds were all the rest he got. Moments later, the front door blew open – breaching charges, most likely – and Remnant soldiers invaded.

They rushed forward, weapons raised and firing. Bullets ripped into the filing cabinets, tore apart the desks, exploded computer monitors, and sent shredded paper fluttering into the air like confetti.

Stone and the deputies returned fire, guns blazing. The roar was deafening inside the close-quarter confines of the station. Men died in a salvo of blood, smoke, and steel. Their corpses fell and were trampled by the men behind them as The Remnant kept on coming. They had nowhere else to go. Blake had put them in a desperate position where their only choice was to succeed at the mission or die trying.

Stone shot a man in the chest, kicking him off his feet with a gaping hole in his heart. He racked the bolt as fast as he could even as his eyes scanned the enemy mob, looking for Blake. No sign of the bastard yet. Probably still hiding behind his men, using them for cannon fodder to protect himself.

A smoke grenade arced through the burning window.

Shit!

The flash-bang device exploded like the crack of doom. Smoke billowed through the room like a thousand ghosts unleashed. Gunfire crackled, muzzle flashes strobing in the artificial fog as The Remnant soldiers surged forward.

Too many of them. Stone knew if they stood their ground, they would be overrun.

"Fall back!" he shouted, his voice rising over the thunder of the guns.

The deputies scrambled in reverse, shooting as they went to cover their retreat. Off to Stone's right, a deputy named Thune took a bullet to the head and sank without so much as a final cry. Stone snarled a curse. One more death that Blake needed to pay for.

They kept themselves spread out as much as possible as they crowded toward the back of the office area, bullets blistering the air. Some hastily-overturned desks provided minimal fortification for their fallback position.

Another smoke grenade skittered across the floor and detonated.

Screams.

Smoke and shadows broken by muzzle flashes.

The deafening sound of gunfire in an enclosed space.

Violence and agony ruled the moment. Men died and lives were lost. Through the smoke and haze, The Remnant soldiers were nothing more than silhouettes and shadows. They twisted and shuddered and fell as Stone and his deputies defended their position.

Stone glanced at Sanchez. Teeth gritted, she blazed away with her AR-15, shredding two targets as they attempted a flanking maneuver. The bullets punched the men into a corner and painted the wall behind them with dark splotches of blood.

The gunfire sounded like a heavy metal soundtrack that would never stop. The adrenaline surging through his veins made Stone feel like they had been fighting for hours, not minutes.

Then somebody yelled, "Cavalry's here!"

Through the smoke, Stone glimpsed Bester and her troops sweeping in behind the remaining Remnant soldiers. Pinned down, the enemy still refused to surrender, choosing to die in defiance on their feet.

Three men broke off and dashed for the back door. Sanchez brought one down with a rifle butt to the face. Another deputy buried a bullet in the second man's brain, blowing the corpse sideways so that it bounced off the wall.

But the third man made it to the back door and bolted out into the sunlight. For a half-second, Stone got a good look at the man's face.

Blake.

Stone went after him.

The Remnant leader sprinted across the small lot behind the station. Clearly his leg wound wasn't slowing him down. By the time Stone made it outside, Blake had fired up one of the four-wheelers and shifted into gear.

Stone raised his rifle, got the bastard in his sights, and squeezed the trigger.

Click.

Stone rasped a very un-preacher-like curse, angry at fate, angry at himself, just angry in general.

Blake grinned knowingly and shot out the front tire of the other ATV. Must have been his last bullet; the slide locked back on an empty chamber. Blake tossed it aside and revved the four-wheeler across the bridge and up the hill into the woods. A spray of dirt, snow, and pine needles rooster tailed from the knobby tires.

Stone followed on foot, lungs heaving as he powered his way up the slope to where he had left Rocky. He quickly climbed into the saddle and took off in pursuit, feeling the strength of the Appaloosa stallion surging beneath him.

THIRTY-SIX

BLAKE LEFT behind a trail like a bull through a China shop.

The ATV's tracks through the mud and snow were so visible that a blind man could have followed them. The four-wheeler carved a wide swath as it plowed through the forest into the deeper woods outside the town limits. Rocky instinctively followed the trail, hooves drumming the ground, and Stone kept his situational awareness switched to high. Cornered people are dangerous people.

And make no mistake, Blake was cornered.

The Remnant leader's forces were either dead or arrested. What little remained of his network would be hounded, harried, and brought down by federal law enforcement. The cause to which he had devoted his fortunes and sacrificed his honor was crumbling down around him, forcing him to abandon his men and flee like a whipped dog.

The Remnant might rise again but for right now, it was done.

As the thought passed through Stone's mind, Blake

lunged from behind a massive pine tree, a Ka-Bar knife clenched in his fist.

Stone reached for his Glock but not fast enough to stop the blade from slashing into Rocky's side. The horse bellowed and reared. Stone threw himself from the stallion, the world twisting crazily as he crashed against a tree trunk. Pain flared in his side, and he wondered if he had cracked a rib. He banged his head against a log as he hit the ground and stars pinwheeled across his blurring vision.

Rocky snorted and stumbled from the shock of his wound.

Blake rushed forward like a linebacker going for the game-stopping tackle. Stone managed to drag his pistol out of the holster but the instant it cleared leather, Blake kicked it out of his hand. It tumbled through the air and sank into the snow.

Stone wasted no time lamenting the lost gun. He twisted his hips, rolled onto his side despite the sharp pain punishing his ribs, and lashed out with his foot. The heavy sole of his boot crunched into the side of Blake's knee. The bone didn't snap like he had hoped, but Blake howled in pain and backpedaled.

Stone climbed to his feet, shook his head to clear his vision, and took everything in with one pan-and-scan glance.

He saw Rocky was still on his feet but trembling, head hanging low in pain. Blood streamed from a nasty cut in the horse's flank and reddened the snow beneath him.

Blake loomed a half dozen paces off, knife in one hand, the other clutching the knee Stone had bruised. As Stone stood up, Blake straightened as well.

"I guess this is it, sheriff. This is where we finish it, man to man."

"You're not a man, Blake. You're a murdering piece of shit."

Stone felt an internal shift deep down inside as he moved beyond raw, hot anger to a place of cold, determined calm. Blake was right about one thing – it was time to finish this. The Remnant leader had killed his deputies, wounded others, smuggled military weapons, attacked his station, and conducted a reign of terror all over these mountain roads.

Time for the man to go down, permanently.

As if on cue, Blake attacked with the knife.

Hurting or not, Stone was ready for him.

Blake came in low with a feint, but Stone didn't fall for the bait. He stepped back and swiveled, deflecting the blade, then wheeled around and smashed his elbow into Blake's mouth. He heard the satisfying crunch of smashed teeth. Blake staggered backward but held onto the knife.

Stone pressed forward. Blake clearly had some knife combat training; he didn't just whip the blade back and forth like an amateur. They spent the next minute locked in a deadly dance of slash and parry, stab and block, boots shuffling through the snow.

Blake darted in, knife driving toward Stone's neck in a blur of steel. Stone dodged to the side and countered with a short, hard kick. His boot heel hammered Blake's other knee. No bone snap, but the leg buckled.

As he collapsed, Blake snagged a handful of Stone's coat and tried to drag him down too. Stone pulled away and kicked him again, this time in the side of the head. The blow sent Blake sprawling and Stone's next kick caught him right in the face. Blood burst from his pulped nose to mix with the strawberry-colored spittle drooling from his mangled mouth.

Despite the beat down, Blake kept a firm grip on the

Ka-Bar. Stone had witnessed better warriors than Blake suffer less punishment and drop their blades. It was like the son of a bitch had superglued the knife to his hand.

Stone moved to kick the bastard in the balls and end the fight for good. But Blake shuffled around on the ground faster than anticipated and struck with the blade, aiming to slice open Stone's calf or ankle.

Stone lifted his leg and the slash passed a half-inch under his foot. He stomped down, pinning Blake's wrist to the ground. He heard a crackle-crunch sound as the bones collapsed under his boot heel. Blake screamed as his fingers spasmed open and dropped the knife.

Stone retrieved the Ka-Bar, then removed his boot from Blake's broken wrist and took a couple steps back. "Get up," he said. "I'll give you the dignity of dying on your feet."

The Remnant leader slowly stood up, wobbly from two swollen knees and clutching his wrist, his face a mask of blood. He glared at Stone with the hostile, desperate eyes of a wounded, cornered animal. "This your idea of a fair fight?"

"It's a damn sight better than the chance you gave Drummond," Stone rasped. "And you didn't seem too worried about fair when you were the one holding the knife a minute ago."

Blake seemed to realize talking was a waste of time. He lurched forward, a good deal faster than Stone would have thought possible, given the man's injured knees. Blake's good hand curled into a claw that slashed at Stone's eyes.

Stone blocked the strike and drove the knife into Blake's stomach. With his other hand, he grabbed the back of Blake's neck and jerked him close, burying the blade to the hilt.

The Remnant leader didn't scream this time; just let

out a long, drawn out groan, a miserable sound of pain and resignation that the battle was lost. He clawed feebly again at Stone's eyes, one last-gasp effort. But Stone gave the knife a half twist, turning the blade so that the razored edge now faced up. Blake shuddered like an impaled insect.

Stone felt a coldness deep in his bones that had nothing to do with the winter air. He had a decision to make.

The law or justice?

If he pulled out the knife and summoned an ambulance, Blake would survive the stab wound and live to stand trial. The legal system would have its way and the outcome would be whatever prosecutors, defense attorneys, and judges decided.

If he pulled the knife upward, Blake would bleed out right here in the woods. The court system would be denied its machinations, but primal justice would be served.

For Stone, it wasn't really much of a choice at all.

Face grim and jaw clenched, he dragged the blade upward like he was gutting a deer, opening Blake from belly to breastbone.

Blake screamed as everything inside came out.

But not for long.

THIRTY-SEVEN

"I CAN'T BELIEVE someone would stab Rocky!"

Lizzy's eyes narrowed in anger as she watched Rocky nibble some hay in the corral behind Stone's place. The vet had examined, treated, and bandaged the knife wound on the stallion's flank. It had been a close call, but the horse would be all right. Stone thought of something his father used to say.

"You can't kill me 'til God wants me."

Maybe that was true for horses too.

"Some people are just total jerks," Lizzy said.

"I think this is where I'm supposed to say that all people are God's children," Stone said. "But truth is, some of God's children are assholes."

Lizzy smiled and nodded in agreement. "You said it, preacher." Then she got somber. "I heard you killed the guy. They're saying it was self-defense."

"I did what needed to be done," Stone said, and left it at that.

"... following the ongoing sweep by Federal agents, resulting in the arrests so far of fifteen members of a violent neo-Nazi militia known as The Remnant, including U.S. Army Major General Lyle Kincaid, who supplied the domestic terrorist organization with military weapons. The group was responsible for the armed attack on the Garrison County Sheriff's station last week which resulted in multiple deaths. Next up, traffic with Lester—"

Stone switched off the radio and stared out the window at the courthouse parking lot. It was a trial day and his turn to testify. About as much fun as a root canal. But at least Blake was gone, Rocky was on the mend, and this latest chapter of violence in his life seemed to be coming to a close.

Maybe when he was done testifying, he would take a few days off, see if Holly and Lizzy wanted to take a road trip somewhere. A weekend getaway in Maine or New Hampshire would do them all good.

He exited the Blazer, walked across the parking lot, and rounded the corner to the front of the courthouse. He noticed a row of Harleys lining the street and a small crowd of people gathered on the courthouse steps. As he approached, he spotted Holly talking to Sonny.

"There he is." Sonny turned and nudged Roy, the Children's president.

"Howdy, sheriff." Roy came forward, hand outstretched, a half dozen bikers at his back. Stone warily shook the offered hand as Holly stepped up beside him.

"What are you guys doing here?" Stone asked. The Children sported their usual biker getup, but everyone's jeans were freshly pressed, their hair and beards washed and combed. They looked as spit and polished as possible for patch-wearing road dogs.

"They came to show their support." Holly hooked her arm through his. "Sonny set it up."

"We're damn grateful to you, sheriff," said Roy. "You put that son of a bitch Dorey in jail and busted up The Remnant. Now we can ride the roads again without worrying about getting run down by those bastards."

"You're one of the good guys, Stone," Sonny said. "Balls of steel."

"Damn right," Roy agreed. "You can ride with us anytime."

"Thanks," Stone said. "But I prefer a real horse to a steel one." He pointed at his Stetson. "Comes with the hat."

They all enjoyed a good laugh and then Stone made his way into the building, Holly by his side.

As he turned the corner into the main hallway, he spotted Deputy Sanchez pushing a man in a wheelchair. With a grin and a shake of his head, Stone stepped forward and put his hand on the man's shoulder.

"Valentine, are you supposed to be here?"

"Figured by now you must be missing me something fierce." Valentine grinned back at him. He still looked weak and it would be a long time before he was fit for duty again, but he was clearly getting better.

"He begged me to break him out of the hospital to be here today," Sanchez explained. "I couldn't say no."

"Thanks for coming, both of you." Stone gestured at the courtroom door. "Guess it's game time."

"Good luck." Sanchez pushed Valentine's wheelchair into the courtroom, one of the Children holding the door for them. Then the rest of the group filed in, leaving Stone and Holly alone.

"I wait out here until called," Stone told her. "Court procedure."

"Right." Holly squeezed his arm. "Put Dorey away for

a long time and make sure The Remnant can never rise again."

Stone looked down at her pretty face and thought about telling her that until the world ended, evil would always rise. But then he decided against it and simply said, "I'll see what I can do."

Holly nodded and joined the others in the courtroom. Mason and Slidell were already inside, and Dorey would arrive soon. All of Slidell's bullshit procedural allegations had been refuted by the state and it was time to buckle down to the actual trial.

Stone cooled his heels in the hall until the bailiff called him. He removed his Stetson, walked into the courtroom, and proceeded to the witness stand. He felt Dorey's hostile eyes glaring at him as he passed but ignored him. After being sworn in, Stone took a seat. Slidell stood up and slithered over.

"Sheriff Stone, as an officer of the law, you are aware of the significance of the oath you just took, correct? And the consequences of violating that oath?"

Stone nodded. "I am."

"Excellent. Because far too many law enforcement officials *say* they understand the oath to protect and serve, but in actuality do not. But you… well, good sir, you understand it, thank God." Slidell paused, lips creased in the thinnest of smiles. "Of course, we only have your word on that…"

"Objection," Mason called out. "Defense is badgering the witness."

"Sustained." Judge Jaramillo glowered at Slidell. "Cut the nonsense, counselor, and get on with it."

"Of course, your honor."

There was movement in the rear of the courtroom as the door opened and Bester entered, followed by Spencer. The FBI agent took a seat while Spencer stepped up and handed a folder to Mason. The prosecutor opened it and quickly scanned the contents, his face betraying nothing.

"Counselor." The judge sounded impatient as she speared Mason with a disapproving look. "Is there something you want to tell me?"

"Sorry, your honor." Mason held up the folder. "I have the results of the Attorney General's audit of Sheriff Stone and his department."

Jaramillo's eyebrows shot up. "That was fast. I'd like to take a look. Bailiff, if you please. Mr. Slidell, you may continue." When the folder was passed to her, the judge cracked it open and began reading as Slidell resumed his questioning.

"Sheriff, my client, Mr. Dorey, was subjected to potentially lethal bodily harm while in your care and custody last week. Is that correct?"

"We all were. His buddies attacked the station."

"Unfortunate, yes, but what methodology did you employ to protect his wellbeing?"

"We locked him in a cell and shot as many of his buddies as we could before they shot us."

"And I'm sure you find that to be perfectly reasonable," Slidell replied. "But as I'm sure the Attorney General's audit doubtlessly demonstrates, your department's operations have been questionable for quite some time."

"That's not what this says." Judge Jaramillo waved the folder. "I want both counsels and you two," she pointed at Spencer and Bester, "in my chambers right now."

"All rise!"

Stone and Mason followed the bailiff out the door. Bester moved up beside him as they walked.

"Slidell's about to have a bad day," she said quietly.

"What do you mean?"

"You'll see."

"Wait...how are you involved in the audit?"

Spencer spoke up from behind them. "Bester called in some favors, got this audit wrapped up in days instead of the months it usually takes."

"Didn't want that crap hanging over your head," she explained. "Plus, I figured it would fuck up Slidell's day."

"The state of New York appreciates the assist from our federal partners," Spencer said.

"Anytime," Bester replied with a grin.

They all filed into Judge Jaramillo's chambers, which smelled like some kind of sagebrush potpourri. The judge sat behind her desk, poring over the audit folder. She looked less than happy but at the moment it was difficult to determine the target of her irritation.

"Sheriff Stone," she said. "On behalf of the court, I would like to extend my apologies for the baseless attacks on your character you have suffered in my courtroom at the hands of the defense." She held up the folder. "From what I am reading here, your department – and you in particular – have demonstrated a level of courage and integrity beyond reproach."

Stone didn't let the surprise show on his face. He simply nodded and said, "Just doing our jobs, your honor."

"Now, Mr. Slidell." The judge turned to face the defense attorney. "Let me be clear." She dropped the folder on her desk. "Your claims about Sheriff Stone have turned out to be absolutely baseless. He clearly has the confidence of the FBI and the State Police." She tapped the folder. "And included in this report are commendation letters from municipal, county, and state officials as well as a Deputy Director from the Justice Department and a retired Supreme Court judge."

Stone glanced at Bester. She shrugged innocently as if to say, *Just doing my job.*

Beside him, Mason wore an ear-to-ear grin.

"We are going to go back out there and finish this trial," Judge Jaramillo continued, eyes still fixed on Slidell. "But you will stick to the facts. No more trying to make Sheriff Stone look like the bad guy. If you insist on going down the character assassination road, prepare to have me cut the legs out from under you. Am I clear?"

Slidell looked like a scolded toddler who just had his lollipop taken away for bad behavior. He struggled to pull together the fragments of his broken pride, raised his downcast eyes, and said, "Perfectly clear, your honor."

"Good." The judge rose and checked her watch. "We'll go for another hour, then break for lunch. Because it's taco Tuesday down at Burracho Billy's and I'm starving."

THIRTY-EIGHT

THE DAY ENDED with the defense making a poor showing. The trial would most likely drag on for another day or two but things weren't looking promising for Slidell or, by extension, Dorey. Stone said goodbye to Sanchez and Valentine as the Children roared off on their Harleys.

"I don't know about you guys," he said, turning to Holly, Bester, and Spencer, "but I could go for a drink. First round's on me."

"Free booze?" Spencer said. "What kind of cop would I be if I said no to that?"

"Sounds good." Bester nudged Holly with an elbow and winked. "Gonna let me buy you a drink, pretty lady?"

"As long as you don't try to spike it and take me home," she said with a smile.

They headed down to the Jack Lumber and grabbed a table. Grizzle came out from behind the bar to personally take their orders, giving Stone a slap on the back with his scarred face stretched in a warm, welcoming grin. He returned a few minutes later with a Jack and Coke – easy on the Jack, lots of ice – for Stone, a white wine for Holly, a beer for Spencer, and a mojito for Bester.

"Never figured you for a Hemingway fan," Stone said, eyeballing Bester's cocktail.

"I'm not. I'm just a fan of his drinking habits. Folks, a toast. To Sheriff Lucas Stone. Part-time preacher, full-time law dog, and all-the-time badass." She hoisted her glass. "Long may he ride."

One drink became three, except for Stone who had a firm two-drink limit. They talked and laughed for an hour before Spencer excused himself to head for home. The remaining three finished their drinks, waved to Grizzle, and drifted out to the parking lot.

"Well, Stone." Bester jangled her car keys in her fist. "We're smoking out bits of The Remnant one rat nest at a time. We couldn't have done it without you. I'll make sure you get some kind of official Bureau recognition."

"Happy hunting." Stone extended his hand. "Thanks for everything, Bester. I owe you one."

"Yeah, you do. And don't worry, I'll call in the favor someday." She smiled and shook his hand.

"You call, I'll be there."

Bester turned to Holly. "Guess this is goodbye. Hopefully our paths cross again at some point."

"Thanks, Taryn. You really came through for us. For this town." Holly stepped forward and without warning, wrapped the FBI agent in a tight embrace and gave her a long, lingering kiss on the lips.

"What was that for?" Bester asked when it was over, a little breathless.

"That's for bringing him home safe to me." She smiled, stepped back, and raised a finger. "Just a one-time thing. No repeats."

"That's a shame, because I'd go through hell for

another one of those." She winked at Stone. "You should try it someday, preacher."

Stone gave her a crooked smile, thinking, *Someday, maybe I will.*

Bester waved and started walking away. "Been fun, guys. 'Til next time."

Stone watched as she headed to her car, walking a little unsteadily. Something told him it wasn't just the booze.

THIRTY-NINE

A WEEK LATER, Stone guided Rocky through the woods, pushing the Appaloosa stallion up the mountain using narrow game paths rather than the main hiking trail that led up to the falls. The air boasted a crisp bite, but the brilliant sunlight softened the brittle edge.

About halfway up a steep ridge, they reached a break in the trees, a small clearing on top of a stone ledge that jutted from the earth like a gray finger. Stone reined the horse to a halt and turned to survey the scenery. Way down below, he could see his house, the ribbon of Route 3 snaking across the rugged country, and further off, the smudged outlines of Whisper Falls.

He just sat there for a while, thinking about things.

At some point, probably sooner rather than later, he would need to figure out his relationship with Holly. He still had shields up around his heart, put in place after the death of his daughter and subsequent divorce. Keeping his emotional distance from romantic entanglements had seemed like the best way to avoid getting hurt again.

"Time to face it, Rocky," he said, patting the stallion's neck. "I've got some trust issues."

Maybe he could work at overcoming them. Or maybe in matters of the heart, he would never again know peace. But one thing was for sure – the thought of Holly with someone else left him deeply unsettled.

He turned his thoughts elsewhere. Staring off into the distance, he pondered his place in this world. Even up here in High Peaks country, change was on the rise as a younger generation found its voice and ushered in new ideas, new customs, new ways of thinking.

To them, Stone was a relic of a bygone age, his cowboy hat, six-shooter, badge, and Bible making him a throwback dinosaur that no longer belonged in the modern world. He was a man holding to a code of justice that had long gone out of style.

But he didn't much care what others thought. That "cowboy code" was his and nobody could make him bend. Some people understood, some did not. He was fine either way.

His father had once told him that the world would always need cowboys.

Stone prayed to God that was true.

A LOOK AT: THE ASSASSIN'S PRAYER
THE ASSASSINS BOOK ONE

HARD-HITTING ACTION WITH A WHOLE LOT OF HEART.

Burned by the betrayal of his best friend and embittered by the tragic death of his wife, former government assassin Gabriel Asher becomes a freelance gun-for-hire, trying hard to bury the past beneath a violent sea of bullets, blood, and booze.

But some sins refuse to stay buried…

Asher soon finds himself targeted by Black Talon, a brutal kill-team from his past led by the ruthless and legendary Colonel Macklin. Asher just wants to be left alone but when fate thrusts an ex-lover back into his life and she is caught up in the crossfire, Asher unleashes a take-no-prisoners war against his enemies. As the guns thunder and the bodies bite the dust, he finds the scars on his soul being ripped wide open.

With its full-throttle pace, hard-hitting action, and heart-wrenching emotion, The Assassin's Prayer is a relentless tale of redemption for those who know that sometimes bullets speak louder than words.

Publisher's Note: The Assassin's Prayer has been updated with new characters, major revisions, and an exhilarating new ending in this brand-new edition.

AVAILABLE NOW

ABOUT THE AUTHOR

Mark Allen was raised by an ancient clan of ruthless ninjas and now that he has revealed this dark secret, he will most likely be dead by tomorrow for breaking the sacred oath of silence. The ninjas take this stuff very seriously.

When not practicing his shuriken-throwing techniques or browsing flea markets for a new katana, Mark writes action fiction. He prefers his pose to pack a punch, likes his heroes to sport twin Micro-Uzis a la Chuck Norris in Invasion USA, and firmly believes there is no such thing as too many headshots in a novel.

He started writing "guns 'n' guts" (his term for the action genre) at the not-so-tender age of 16 and soon won his first regional short story contest. His debut action novel, The Assassin's Prayer, was optioned by Showtime for a direct-to-cable movie. When that didn't pan out, he published the book on Amazon to great success, moving over 10,000 copies in its first year, thanks to its visceral combination of raw, redemptive drama mixed with unflinching violence.

Now, as part of the Wolfpack team, Mark Allen looks forward to bringing his bloody brand of gun-slinging, bullet-blasting mayhem to the action-reading masses.

Mark currently resides in the Adirondack Mountains of upstate New York with a wife who doubts his ninja skills because he's always slicing his fingers while chop-ping veggies, two daughters who refuse to take tae kwon do, let alone ninjitsu, and enough firepower to ensure that he is never bothered by door-to-door salesmen.